PRAISE FOR TAMARA GRANTHAM

"Part Twilight, part Beauty and the Beast, readers will eat up the lush settings, mystery, and romance of Never Call Me Vampire."

-ANGELA LARKIN, CO-AUTHOR OF THE BEYOND SERIES

"I found Never Call Me Vampire mesmerizing and worth reading in one sitting. Tamara Grantham takes the enchanting theme of vampires and builds on their reputation and thrilling mystique to create a novel that will haunt you until it is finished."

-PEGGY JO WIPF, READERS FAVORITE

"[T]his story works well because of the value that Tamara Grantham adds to the theme, which makes it hard to put down once you start reading."

TAMARA GRANTHAM

-VINCENT DUBLADO

"A sparkling fantasy."

-KIRKUS REVIEWS (FOR THE WITCH'S TOWER)

"Never Call Me Vampire...is the amazing start of a promising para-
normal series. If you've been longing for a good vampire novel with a
new spin, your search ends here."
-TAMMY RUGGLES

Don't Blame the Chosen One

Tamara Grantham

DREAM•GARTEN
Press

Dream Garten Press

Book Cover by Shawnda Craig

Edits by Rachel Hatchcock and Alicia Dean

First edition 2023

To my uncle Edward. My biggest fan.

"Everything you want is on the other side of fear."

-Jack Canfield

Contents

Chapter 1
SPOILER ALERT

S poiler alert: I'm not the Chosen One. My grandpa broke the news to me. Am I disappointed? Maybe. But I haven't let that little roadblock stop me from becoming the best *pretend* Chosen One the world has ever seen. This brings me to my current situation: nearly getting killed with my own sword.

Fandalore stabbed at me with the blade of the Hero's sword. I barely managed to deflect his blow. The wizard's blue robes swallowed his thin frame, and his skinny arms stuck out from his sleeves like twigs. He grasped the hilt of the Hero's sword with both of his bony hands, then he swung again. I leapt back, lost my balance, and landed squarely on my tailbone, onto the root of a tree root, no less.

"Ouch," I winced, my backside aching as I stared at the thick blanket of gray clouds through the swaying limbs of a willow tree, the scent of rain perfuming the air.

My sword, Schubert, laughed as I gripped the pommel.

"Tallyho," he hooted. "Remarkable form, Mr. Tevyn. I suppose this move was called the bottom buster. Or perhaps the blotched backside? Maybe the buttocks bash—"

"That's enough." I squeezed the hilt, which usually quieted him, but he kept laughing, although a little more quietly.

Fandalore gave a longsuffering sigh as he stood over me, his leathery face blocking the sky. His white beard was so long, its bushy tail tickled my nose. One of his caterpillar eyebrows rose as he stared at me, then pointed a finger in my face.

"Pay attention, young whelp," he said in his wheezy, nasal voice. "What if that had been the Wraith King's attack?"

"If that had been the Wraith King's attack," I said through clenched teeth, "then I wouldn't have been using this pretend piece of scrap metal." I gripped Schubert's hilt and wiggled it in the air.

"*Scrap metal?*" Schubert gasped. "Pardon me, but perhaps I've never told you of my exploits during the reign of King Kaladin, when a passing caravan paid four thousand gold pieces for me. Yes, you heard right. Me. For four-thousand pieces. I'm far from scrap metal, you ungrateful child. Of course, I may have been described as the true Hero's sword by the band of thieves who happened to steal me—and, as you know, I look very much like the real one—but that's hardly the point."

"Your sword makes little difference," Fandalore added after Schubert's rant. "It's your form that needs improvement. Balance. That's the difference between life and death."

I got to my feet, my muscles stiff and protesting. We stood on a grassy hill overlooking Elderhurst castle. The crumbling structure's gray stones matched the clouds of the same color. "How am I supposed to keep my balance *or* my concentration when I'm being yelled at by you and my sword?" I demanded.

"Distractions during a battle with the Wraith King will be far worse," Fandalore said gravely, a hint of seriousness in his usually carefree voice.

"Maybe," I admitted, my shoulders slumped as I grasped the necklace around my neck. The enchanted tree pendant was black except for a gray spot at the tree's center. My stomach sickened at the sight of it.

The tree was enchanted to tell me the status of my sister Kyrie's health. If it turned completely black, it meant... well... I couldn't even think the word. I couldn't imagine a world without my sister in it. If I lost her, what became of my family?

Instead of pondering the implications of a world without Kyrie, I tucked the tree pendant underneath my shirt, then I glanced at my friends to distract me. Luria and Maharani waited under a nearby tree. Maharani sat polishing his new shield. Its decoration of a tree with gracefully arching branches gleamed as brightly as a mirror.

He gave me an encouraging smile. The wind gusted, making his poofy hair blow against his set of ram's horns. Luria stood nearby and held her newly acquired staff. Her red-and-black scaled face contorted with concentration as she pointed the wand at the ground, muttering one curse after another.

"This staff is so useless." Purple crystals glittered from its top as she stabbed the tip into the ground.

"Well..." Maharani said. "That *is* its name, right? Staff of Uselessness?"

She shot him a dark glare, but he ignored her contemptuous look and continued polishing his shield. At least one of us was having success with our new weapon.

"Why can't I use the real sword?" I demanded of Fandalore, shaking my current sword.

"Because you must learn correct form first," he answered. "And discipline. And movement. And flourishes once you've got the rest." He whipped the sword through the air with an exaggerated swagger.

"Ugg..." I grumbled. "I'm not even the real Chosen One. Everyone knows it. Why am I even learning sword fighting?"

"Because you pulled the sword from the stone," Fandalore admonished.

"Which means what?"

"Which means you're willing to sacrifice whatever it takes to defeat the Wraith King. You sacrificed that which was most dear to you to get this sword, didn't you?"

My hand brushed over my empty pocket where I usually kept Grandpa's watch. The empty fabric reminded me of what wasn't there, and a hollow feeling sank straight through me. "Yes," I answered, swallowing hard. "I did."

"Then the sword knows you're worthy of something," Fandalore said. "It may not be in defeating the Wraith King, but it's surely something special."

"Like becoming the Alderfell champion of backside brutality," my sword chimed in, and I resisted the urge to chunk it across the field.

Behind me came the sound of a giant shifting its weight, and a faint smell of brimstone filled the air. I turned to see a huge black dragon lumbering toward us. Thimblethorn shuffled his weight across the field, the old castle in the distance, as his yellow eyes focused on us.

"Castle kitchens just ran out of lamb chops," he announced, licking his lips with a long, thin tongue. "They were a far cry from cheeseburgers, I tell you. But a dragon must take whatever sustenance is available."

"Sorry about that," I said, hunching my shoulders.

He waved a claw dismissively through the air. "No need to apologize. I'm sure you'll fulfill the bargain when you have the ability."

"Yeah," I answered halfheartedly. The only problem was that we were planning to travel straight to the Dragon Wraith Mountains. I doubted we'd have many prospects for obtaining cheeseburgers along the way, as the road to the mountains was nothing but wasteland. I only hoped he had a hearty appetite for foraged greens.

"I think I see the problem here," Fandalore said, rubbing his chin and giving me a critical look. "It's very difficult for one to be a convincing Chosen One without one crucial thing—something you're missing, young pup."

"What do you mean?" I asked, raising one eyebrow. "I've got the sword, the dragon. I've even got you, the wizard—the real one."

"Yes, but there is one thing that all Chosen Heroes have in common. Something you're lacking."

"I can tell you," Schubert started. "I've made a list of one-hundred-and-one items that he's lack—"

I squeezed the hilt so hard, my fingers ached. "Don't even start."

"It's not anything tangible, young one," Fandalore said. "Not something you can get at a zoo or find in a castle."

I got the feeling he was leading me along for dramatic effect. "Would you just tell me?" I asked. "Please?" I added.

"Well, if you must know..." he said with a severe frown, as if he were annoyed I'd asked the question before allowing a theatrical lead-up to the grand reveal. "It's a scar."

I narrowed my eyes. "A scar?"

"Why, yes. Every great hero carries a scar. On the forehead, usually, that's the best place to display it, of course. A hero's scar can also be found anywhere really, on the shoulder, an ankle, sometimes the back of the neck. Where would you like yours?" He pointed the tip of the sword in my face. "I'll be happy to give you one, of course. A scar made by a wizard with the Hero's sword would be a noble mark indeed. I would suggest the forehead, but it's your choice." He brushed a clump of blond hair away from my forehead with the tip of the sword.

"No thanks." I swatted the sword away. "I'd rather pick up a scar the traditional way."

"Ah yes," he said with a nod. "In a battle to the death? That would be your only option as you weren't naturally born with a mark."

"Yeah." I rubbed my neck. "Something like that. Umm anyway..." I cleared my throat. "Maybe I should continue my training?" I didn't say it out loud, but I'd rather train with him any day than allow him to leave a permanent scar on me. He wasn't really serious about that, was he?

"If you wish." Fandalore stood as straight as his stooped shoulders would allow. "However, all this talk of scars reminds me of something. Have you ever heard of the Scared Knights of Evalon?"

"*Scared* knights?" I questioned.

"Scared, yes," he answered with a vigorous nod.

"You don't mean Scarred?" I asked. "Surely they're not called Scared."

Fandalore wrinkled his browed, glanced at the sky, then spelled out loud... "S-C-A-R-E-D... no S-C-A-R-R-E-D... was it one R or two?" He twisted his beard around his finger. "Well, the truth is, these Knights of Evalon, we'll call them, either Scared or Scarred... are the premier knights who have trained every young hero starting with Kaladin the Brave. They're the best, and an absolute must for your training." He heaved a sigh. "They're not close, unfortunately. More than ten days travel from here if one goes on foot."

"By foot?" Maharani chimed in. "We already took the Path of Ellory by foot. Surely, we don't have to do it again?"

"Of course, we must," Fandalore said with a huff. "It's the journey that strengthens the hero. By foot we must go. To the northwest, I believe. Ruins of Evalon." He scratched his chin.

"The northwest?" Luria questioned. "That's a little vague, don't you think?"

"The winged train runs to the northwest," Maharani said as he pulled his map from his cloak's pocket. He unrolled the parchment and scanned the page. "Yes, the Solar Courier line runs northwest. It doesn't go straight to Evalon, but it gets close."

I crossed to where my cousin sat and glanced at his map. "Zappers, you're right."

Fandalore placed his fists on his bony hips. "What's the point of becoming a Chosen hero if you elect to remain soft by taking public transportation? No trains."

"But..." Maharani argued.

"And no buts," Fandalore said.

Thimblethorn shook out his wings. "Another trek by foot. Must I go? I really do have a rough time of traveling. Quite bad on the joints, you know. Gives me the worst ache in my knees."

"Of course you must go," Fandalore argued. "What is a Chosen One without his dragon?"

"I hear the trains are equipped with flatbed cars that would accommodate Thimblethorn," Maharani said. "I mean, if we decide to use them."

"Yeah," I chimed in. "And they serve meals onboard, too. I mean, it's not the best food, but it beats trail mix and wild greens."

"No, no, no." Fandalore waved his skinny arms. "You aren't listening to me. Did any of the past Chosen Heroes use trains to travel? I think not."

"But they didn't even have trains back then," I argued. "I bet if they did, they would have used them."

"Gordy's right," Maharani said.

"*Tevyn*," Luria corrected.

"Right. Tevyn." Maharani scratched his chin. "I keep forgetting to use your Chosen One name."

"It's okay," I said. "Honestly, I don't really feel like a Tevyn anymore. I feel more like a Gordy."

"So," my cousin said with one eyebrow raised. "You don't want us to call you Tevyn?"

I glanced at the true Hero's sword, then back to the fake one. I didn't want to be a fake any longer. If I was really taking the path to defeat the Wraith King, I would do it as myself.

"Call me Gordy," I answered. "Just Gordy."

My friends nodded, and I absentmindedly grasped the pendant around my neck and rubbed the metal branches. I couldn't help but envision what Kyrie looked like right now. She was probably lying on the couch, her skin as white as parchment paper. In my imagination, her eyes were closed, and she was peacefully sleeping, because I couldn't bear to imagine her as she really was—blind and terrified.

I hadn't gotten any word from my mom recently. As far as I knew, my dad was still missing after the attack at the magical power plant. If I thought of how much my family was suffering, I would fall apart. So, instead, I took a deep breath and pushed my fears aside.

Thunder rumbled in the distance with an ominous, drawn-out wail, and the wind carried the scent of rain. Leaves rustled in the trees overhead.

"Wherever we're going," I said, looking anxiously at the darkening clouds, "we should probably go soon."

Maharani glanced back at the Elderhurst ruins, his gaze pensive, his dark eyes wide and his face pinched with worry. "Are we sure we're ready?"

"I'm ready," Luria stated with her usual matter-of-fact tone, a note of finality in her voice. "Even if I don't know how use this useless thing." She jabbed the staff on the ground before coming to stand by me. "Let's go."

Maharani examined his map. "We can take this path to the north-west until we find this road." He pointed to a snaking line on the parchment. "That will take us to the Forest of Marlock's Doom where we can take this path the rest of the way to the Scared Knight's castle."

"Scared Knights," I mumbled under my breath. "Silliest name ever."

"What about Marlock's Doom?" Luria asked. "That doesn't sound too inviting, does it?" She scrunched her brow, the smooth red-and-black scales on her face glistening as a ray of sunlight broke free from the clouds. Her dark glossy hair hung loosely over her shoulders, and her ram-like horns curved gracefully from her head. I couldn't decide if I was terrified of her, or maybe the teeniest bit attracted. One thing I knew, Luria wasn't someone you took lightly. I was glad she was on our side.

"Onward," Fandalore shouted, pointing the way to the northwest. "The Scared Knights await."

Chapter 2

NEVER TAKE A DRAGON FOR GRANTED

Mud squished beneath my boots. It had been raining off and on for the last hour, and I was certain I'd never been more soaked in my life. Luria and Maharani looked about as miserable as me. Even Fandalore had stopped chirping about how great it was to travel by foot. The only member of our group not bothered by the weather was Thimblethorn.

He plodded along, occasionally shaking out his wings, but otherwise not complaining. The rain finally let up as we crested a hill, and the evening sun broke through the clouds. Long streaks of pink and purple reminded me of sword blades cutting through the sky. Except for a thread of silver winding above the hilltops, which must have been the sky train's rail, nothing but fields and forest stretched to the horizon.

My heart sank. "I guess we should make camp before nightfall."

"Yeah," the others agreed, although their voices sounded as dejected as mine. What I wouldn't give for a warm fire and a couch in front of my magi-box.

"Uh, Gordy?" Maharani asked. "We don't have a tent, or much to eat, or even dry firewood."

I glanced around the hilltop. A few scraggly trees stood out like skeletons against the darkening sky. Their wood had turned black from being soaked in the rain. The few sticks and brambles covering the ground were just as soaked, and I poked at a branch with my toe. The prospect of sleeping in wet clothes sounded just about as fun as having a conversation with Schubert about my one-hundred-and-one faults.

I glanced at my friends standing around me, their faces dejected. It had been my plan to go on this quest, and I felt responsible for their current state of misery. No tent. No inn in sight. What were we supposed to do?

Thimblethorn heaved a mighty yawn, showing his mouth full of teeth, and I snapped my fingers.

"Zappers, why didn't I think of it sooner?" I asked.

"Think of what?" Luria asked with one eyebrow raised.

"Thimblethorn's wings. He can stretch one out and make us a tent. Plus, he can use his dragon's breath to start a fire. I remember reading about how Khamron used his dragon for shelter and fire on one of his adventures."

"It's not a bad idea," Luria admitted. "But does Thimblethorn know how to breathe fire?"

"Of course, he does," I answered, glancing at the big dragon out of the corner of my eye. "I think," I added.

"Tut, tut..." Thimblethorn scratched his chest with a long, curving claw. "Sadly, I was never allowed to breathe fire while living in the zoo. Legal reasons, of course. Wouldn't want to burn the patrons."

"But you're not in the zoo anymore," I pointed out. "And we're all soaking wet and need to get dry."

"You're right," Thimblethorn admitted. "But I hardly think it's a good idea to break the rules. I can't afford to be sold to another zoo—or—wizards' forbid, be donated to the circus." He shuddered.

"But you won't be breaking the zoo's rules because you're not at the zoo. We're in charge of you now, and if we say it's okay to breathe fire, then I promise you won't get into trouble."

Thimblethorn only gave me a sidelong glance.

"Thimblethorn," Luria said with a chiding tone. "If you won't fly and you won't fight—*and* you won't use your fire, then what's the point of bringing you on this quest?"

He only sniffed and stuck his snout in the air.

I shivered and rubbed my arms for warmth. My toes had gone numb hours ago, and I couldn't feel my nose and ears anymore. Looking around, I couldn't spot a single piece of dry wood anywhere. What could I say to convince Thimblethorn to use his fire and help us out?

"I've got an idea," Maharani said, reaching into his bag. He removed a sandwich wrapped in brown paper. "I got this at the castle food court, and I was planning to save it for our dinner tonight, but..." He held it out. "I know you're probably hungrier than us. It's yours if you'll create a fire."

"Hmm..." He hesitated, looking with wide, greedy eyes at the sandwich.

"It's not a cheeseburger, but it's ham and cheddar, and I just bought it this morning, so it's still sort of fresh."

He straightened his long neck. "White or wheat?"

Paper crinkled as Maharani peeked under the wrapping. "White. Sourdough, I think."

"Very well." Thimblethorn snatched the sandwich out of my cousin's hands. He delicately unwrapped it before stuffing the food in his mouth. "Quite good," he said between bites. "Lettuce is a bit soggy, but the ham is savory. Not bad at all. Ah, yes." He pounded his chest and let out a short burp. "Just the thing a hungry dragon needs to fuel a robust breath of fire."

Maharani jabbed me playfully with his elbow and gave me an encouraging smile.

"*Good job, cuz,*" I mouthed to him.

"Well..." Thimblethorn motioned to the trees around us. "You'll need to gather the wood. I can't set the whole forest on fire, now, can I?"

My friends and I made quick work of gathering soggy logs and sticks, then placing them in a heap on the rain-soaked ground. When we'd made a large pile, Thimblethorn gave it a critical eye.

"Is that enough wood to start a fire?" I asked.

"Yes, it should do. But I will warn you..." He waggled a claw in our faces. "Once you're under the shelter of my wing, you'd better not be planning to allow a fire beneath it." He gave a small flap, sending a whoosh of humid air into our faces.

"We understand," I said, then glanced around our camp. "Uhh... has anyone seen Fandalore?"

Luria and Maharani glanced around.

"I haven't seen him for a while," Maharani said, and Luria agreed.

"I guess we'll have to get used to that," I admitted. "In my books, wizards were always wandering off for some reason or another." I scratched my chin. "Never really knew why, either. Secret wizard business, I guess."

"Then I think it's a waste of time to worry about him," Luria said. "Besides, he's how old? I'm pretty sure he can take care of himself, especially since he's lived this long. Still... Thimblethorn..." she glanced up and addressed the dragon. "Go ahead and start the fire. If Fandalore is out wandering somewhere, seeing a fire should help him find us."

"Good idea," I said.

The dragon inhaled a giant breath, then opened his mouth wide. Golden-orange flames streamed out, their heat warming my face, until it caught the pile of wood on fire. Wet wood crackled and steamed. Soon, the three of us sat around the bonfire with our hands outstretched.

"Well, here you are," Fandalore announced in a booming voice as he strode into camp.

"Where were you?" I asked.

He looked affronted. "Where was I?" he repeated. "You of all people should know never to ask a wizard about his business. Where a wizard goes is our own affair—a mystery that more often than not gets resolved in due time. Now." He rubbed his hands together by the fire. "What's for dinner?"

"Eh…" I glanced at my friends. "Thimblethorn ate it already."

I expected the wizard to throw a fit and tell us what a poor job we were doing with our survival skills on this quest, but he only shrugged and sat on a log by the fire. Maybe he was used to quests where no one had food.

After the fire dwindled, Thimblethorn curled up nearby, and we squeezed under one of his wings. It wasn't nearly as comfortable or as roomy as I'd imagined, and the ground was still wet, which made sleeping almost impossible. Sticks poked my back, and I couldn't stop shivering. It rained off and on through the night, and I gave up trying to sleep and instead listened to the drops pattering Thimblethorn's wing.

When morning finally arrived, the sky was a dark gunmetal gray, and the chilly, humid air made my clothes stick to my skin. In addition to an empty stomach, I reeked of sour sweat. All I could think about was taking a warm shower, then wearing a fresh pair of soft pajamas, followed by nineteen hours of sleep buried under my covers in my bed back home. What I wouldn't give to be back there right now. Why didn't my books ever mention how completely miserable it was to sleep outdoors?

I hefted my backpack and slung one strap over my shoulder. My scrying screen sat inside, although the magic hadn't been working for a while now. What would Mom have to say if I called her? Had they found Dad yet? How was Kyrie?

Maharani brushed past me with a blank gaze. He looked just about as dismal as me. Dark circles shadowed his eyes, and brambles stuck out from his tangled hair. Luria stood under a nearby tree with an equally gloomy expression. When we set off walking down the trail, I almost called the whole adventure off. The only thing that kept me moving forward was the pendant around my neck, which I clutched until the branches left red marks on my skin. I tried not to focus on the color of the tree, which was completely black except for a pinprick of gray at its center.

Hours later, after the sky had lightened, and the last of the rain-clouds drifted away, we left the shelter of the forest. We hiked over an open, hilly plain and down to a dirt road that connected with another larger roadway paved in cobblestones. A few people pulling handcarts passed us by, giving guarded glances at our enormous black dragon.

A stone signpost rose crookedly from the ground. The words SO-LAR COURIER AHEAD had been etched into the granite cross post. Above, a silver thread of magic glittered across the sky. Bullet-shaped vehicles sped down the levitating ribbon, making a zinging sound as they passed. They created a gust of wind that blew over the long stalks of brown grass surrounding us.

"Look," Maharani pointed. "The Solar Courier."

"How's it still working?" I asked.

"I guess it's got a magical generator of some sort," Maharani answered.

The train slowed as it neared the edge of the horizon, then stopped. Below it, I spotted a square stone building that resembled a castle tower. I could see a few people climbing up the tower to get to the train, though from this vantage point, they looked like little ants.

I looked longingly at the train and at the people boarding it. Luria and Maharani stood beside me, and we all stood staring at the train with mouths open and faraway expressions.

"Well." Fandalore clapped his hands. "It's time, then."

"Time?" I asked.

"Time to take the train," he announced.

"You can't be serious," Luria protested. "Now? After we've slept on the soaking wet ground and trudged halfway across Alderfell? Why couldn't you have agreed to the train yesterday?"

Fandalore shot her a look of annoyance. "An old wizard forgets, of course."

"Forgets what?" I asked.

"All of this." He shook out his robes where a layer of stickers stuck to the hem, and dried mud clung to the soles of his boots. "This misery. So." He pointed his finger at the sky. "We're taking the rails."

I almost questioned him on why he'd given us such a long lecture about the journey making you stronger and all that blah blah, but I decided to keep quiet. I couldn't risk making him mad and changing his mind.

My friends shot me confused glances, but none of us questioned the old wizard as we made our way down the road and to the train outpost. When we finally arrived at the station, we bought tickets with what was left of our money. It cost double to pay for a flatbed for Thimblethorn, which left us with only a few coins left to our name.

I tried not to ponder it too much. Maybe Fandalore could do a few magic tricks and earn some extra money at some point.

All I cared was that I would get to sit down on an actual cushion and sleep for the next several hours.

After boarding the train, my friends and I found an empty compartment and got situated.

"I've never been on a train like this before," Luria said as we stood in the circular compartment with cushioned benches ringing the walls, and a small table in the center. She looked from the cushioned benches to the magi-screen hovering overhead. "You can watch shows while you ride?"

"Don't get too excited," Maharani cautioned. "They usually play the news or something boring."

"Doesn't bother me." I plopped onto a seat and rested my feet on the circular table. "Anything beats being outdoors right now."

Maharani and Luria sat on either side of me. Fandalore had gone missing again, and no one bothered to mention it. Maybe we were all secretly grateful he wasn't hanging around and offering his advice.

"I hope Thimblethorn is okay," Luria mused as she glanced out the window.

"I'm sure he's fine," Maharani offered. "Did you see how happy he was when he curled up on the flatbed?"

The train started with a lurch, and I glanced outside our window. The track rose a hundred feet in the air and was held up by the silver glow of a magical spell. Below us spanned brown grass and a few knobby trees, and I could just make out the road where we'd been traveling that looked like a winding ribbon over the countryside.

"I could get used to this," I said as I propped my hands behind my head. I wasn't sure I'd ever been happier to be inside a train and off my feet. The magi-box inside our compartment crackled with purple static, and a news broadcast started playing. I half listened. Most of it was old news. The Wraith King had escaped. The magical factory in Kroy Wren had been attacked. Possessed crows were everywhere. I dozed until Maharani gave me a tap on my shoulder.

"What's up?" I startled awake and wiped a bead of drool from my mouth.

"Check this out." Maharani pointed to the screen.

A boy about my age sat in an interview with a newscaster. The boy was exceptionally good looking: perfectly straight teeth, silky blond hair that fell neatly to his chin, and striking blue eyes. But his smile seemed odd—fake almost—and he laughed a little too hard at the joke the newscaster was telling.

"But seriously..." the newscaster said, a man with dark hair so shiny you could have seen your reflection in it. "You're an actual orphan from a small village? Your parents mysteriously disappeared when you were a baby, you can talk to magical swords... *and* you can track your lineage to royalty? It almost sounds too good to be true."

"But it's the truth." The boy spread his hands and gave a wide grin, one that showed his dazzling white teeth. "Not too hard to believe when you realize I'm the Chosen Hero."

I bolted straight in my seat. "Wha—?"

Maharani and Luria shushed me.

"If that's the case," the newscaster said dubiously, although he maintained a professional tone. "Then why didn't the Wraith King do away with you when he was first awakened, just as he did to all those other orphan boys he suspected of becoming Chosen Heroes?"

"Simple," the boy answered. "He missed someone." He pointed to his chest. "He missed me."

The scene faded and was followed by a shot of the boy practicing sword fighting in a picturesque field. As he swished the sword through the air, a voiceover played.

"His name is Alexander Bravestone," said a booming, important-sounding voice. "You'll want to remember it, because he might very well be the boy to save us all. He's been practicing sword fighting since he was a toddler, although as an apprentice blacksmith, he wasn't always allowed to do it. Now, he's ready to take his skills to the next level. After being discovered by a great wizard rumored to be Fandalore himself, and tracking down a rare breed of Opalescent dragon, his next quest puts him on a more dangerous path. For now, Alexander maintains that the world has no need to worry about the Wraith King, and we tend to believe him."

"I'll take care of him," Alexander said on screen with a flash of his smile. The scene switched to a newsroom where the newscaster with the shiny hair sat at a table beside an elven woman wearing a business suit.

"So, it's all true?" the woman asked.

"Yes," the man answered. "I can confirm it's true. And I can tell you, Jen. He's an impressive kid. I had my doubts at first, of course. But after spending time with him, I think the defeat of the Wraith King is only a matter of time."

"Wow," Jen said. "Impressive."

The scene switched to a commercial about gummy Trollsters, and I sat back, my mind reeling and my stomach sour.

"This is... unexpected," Maharani said hesitantly.

"That's an understatement." I laughed bitterly.

"He's a complete fraud." Luria threw her hands in the air.

"Well, yeah," I said. "That's obvious. His face is made for the screen. And he's obviously been coached. 'He missed someone. He missed me.'" I quoted in a mocking tone. "Please. He didn't come up with that on his own."

"Yeah, but that's not what I meant," Luria clarified. "He's not even doing this the right way. He didn't mention anything about taking the path of Ellory. Everyone knows the only way to get an Opal dragon is to buy one from breeders or collectors, and that takes thousands of coins. I seriously doubt he bought one all by himself. And his wizard? Fandalore? We all know he's a fake."

"*We* might know that." I said. "But no one else does."

"True." Maharani nodded. "Plus, he doesn't have a sword—at least, not *the* sword."

"He doesn't need it," Luria said irritably.

"What do you mean?" I asked. "Of course, he needs it if he wants to defeat the Wraith King."

"I doubt he's actually intending to battle the Wraith King." Luria tapped her fingers on the windowsill. Outside, the green trees and brown grass were being replaced with craggy rust-colored dunes. "It's more likely he's just a distraction. People are scared and want someone to do something. How much do you want to bet the government is behind this? It's a completely useless gesture, but it makes people feel better to think someone's doing something. It should worry people even more to realize this is the government's best plan."

I sat back in my seat. I'd never felt such a miserable sinking feeling in the pit of my stomach. Only one thing gave me hope: I had the true Hero's sword and Alexander Bravestone didn't.

"But this doesn't make any sense," Maharani said. "Mayor Wren was going along with Gordy's plan to become the Chosen One. At least for a little while. Then she abandoned the plan. Why would she go along with another plan to make *another* fake Chosen One?"

Luria tapped a delicate finger on her chin. "Maybe it wasn't the mayor who agreed to it. Could've been someone higher up. A governor. The president, perhaps. They must all be feeling vulnerable and desperate to look like something's being done."

I rubbed my forehead. "It doesn't matter, anyway. Not to us. This doesn't change anything about our quest. We've got the true sword, the actual Fandalore, and a big dragon. We don't need publicity or acknowledgment. We've got everything we need, and that's the best we can do."

Chapter 3

THE FOREST OF MARLOCK'S DOOM

The train stopped on the outskirts of Marlock's Forest, and I tried not to pay attention to the hairs rising on the back of my neck as we stood on the edge of the trees' shadows. Fandalore had reappeared with bags of boiled peanuts and filets of fried fish wrapped in brown paper, which he passed around to us. "Heroes must have their strength," he explained.

We ate quickly before setting off into the forest. My cousin carefully adjusted his shield which he wore on his back. Luria used her staff as a walking stick, and its purple crystals glowed faintly in the dim light of the forest seeping through the claw-like branches. The amethyst shone over Luria's scaled face and hands and highlighted the worry in her yellow, catlike eyes.

"Are we sure about this?" Thimblethorn asked. Tree branches scraped along his wide body as we paced down the narrow trail. "The air has an oppressive feel. I sense dark magic in this place."

"I agree," Luria said, rubbing her hands over her arms as she glanced up at the skeletal trees. "Something feels wrong."

"Understandable," Fandalore said offhandedly. "It hasn't changed in a thousand years. Places like this stay the same once they've been tainted by dark magic. The Wraith King himself once survived in this forest, performed a terrible ritual that I shan't go into detail about in the presence of you young pups. That was before his defeat by one of the heroes of ages past, though I can't recall which of the heroes defeated him that time. Of course, one must pass through a place like this to get their training. It's all part of the process, you see."

Something moved in the branches beside me, and I jumped before realizing it was only a squirrel. "This place is giving me the creeps."

"Me too," Maharani added. The map crinkled as he held it with shaking hands. "But the good news is that once we're through this forest, we'll be close to the Scared—Scarred—whatever... the Knights' castle. Even so, it could take more than a day to get through the forest, although..." He knit his brow. "There are trails going everywhere. And this is an older map. I'm not even sure which trails still exist. We'll have to be careful not to get lost."

"Wonderful," Thimblethorn huffed ruefully, steam rising from his nostrils.

"Well..." Maharani answered with equal bitterness in his voice. "If you could fly over the forest and inspect the pathways, maybe tell us which one will get us closest to the castle, this job would be a lot easier."

"Fly?" Thimblethorn shuddered. "I've already informed you that it's impossible."

I scanned the dragon's enormous wings. They looked perfectly in shape, and it struck me that maybe the big dragon could fly, but he chose not to.

"Thimblethorn," I said. "What if we were in a fight for our lives, and the only way we could win was for you to fly?"

He sniffed. "That's a ridiculous scenario."

"It doesn't matter," my cousin said with an exaggerated sigh. "We'll keep going down the main pathway until we get to a fork in the road, then we'll turn left." He rolled up the map and stuck it in his pack's pocket.

The forest overshadowed us. Tree branches reached out like a wraith's fingers. The palpable terror was like déjà vu. Like I was re-living one of my dreams where the Wraith King appeared. That same pounding in my heart, that same dread that coiled inside, making my hands clammy and sweat break out all over my skin. Yes, the Wraith King had most definitely been here. I could almost see him through the branches, could feel his eyes on us as we walked deeper into the heart of the forest.

Cawing came from overhead, and I froze. Above us, a cloud of black, winged bodies blocked out the sky.

"Crows," Luria said, her voice fearful as she gripped her staff.

"Maybe they're harmless," my cousin said. "We're in a forest after all. Crows live here, right?"

Fandalore reached for the Hero's sword, pulled it off his belt, and handed it to me. "Well now, here's a test of bravery for you, young novice. If those indeed are possessed crows, you should have no trouble dispatching them."

"You mean killing them?" Luria asked, aghast.

"Yes. I thought *dispatching* was a more refined word, but if we must say it plainly, then killing them it is."

"But they're living creatures," Luria argued. "Even if they are possessed, they can't help it."

"But what if they attack us?" Maharani argued.

"Then we'll use a spell to repel them the same way we did with the other crows that tried attacking us."

"Do you have a spell?" my cousin asked. "Because I lost my dad's weapon in the dungeon, and it was the only thing capable of scaring the crows away."

"Well..." she looked pleadingly at her staff, as if praying that magic would suddenly shoot out of the purple crystals, but no such thing happened. "I'm just saying that killing is wrong. It should be our last resort."

She screamed the last sentence as a whirlwind of feathered bodies descended on the road in front of us, then flew in a cyclone until a small, humanoid shape formed. When the air stilled, my heart stopped.

I looked face to face at my sister.

"Kyrie," I whispered, almost too afraid to speak her name.

Chapter 4
VAL

"Kyrie, is that really you?" My own voice sounded hollow to my ears, like I spoke inside a drum.

The thing that looked like my sister only resembled her a little. Its skin was so pale it looked nearly transparent. Her once golden hair now hung limp and dull down her shoulders. I grasped the pendant around my neck. I shouldn't have been surprised to see it had turned completely black, but the sight of it gave me a jolt, as if I'd been struck by lightning.

My mind reeled as panic set in. I'd worked too hard to save her just for this to happen. How could my little sister be a wraith?

She looked at me with wide, dead eyes that only seemed half lucid. But when she spoke, it was her voice.

"Gordy," she said. "I found you."

"Kyrie," I pleaded. "No. This can't be you."

Luria rested her hand on my shoulder, and I cast her a brief, desperate glance. She'd seen this scene all too many times with first her father and then her brother. How had she managed to deal with it?

"Come with me, Gordy." The thing that looked like Kyrie took a shuffling step forward. "All the pain will go away once you become like the Wraith King."

My heart squeezed so tightly I was surprised it didn't shatter. "Kyrie, no."

"Come," she repeated and stretched out her hand.

Maharani pushed his way in front of me. "Not another step." He gripped his shield in front of him.

Kyrie gave a laugh that sounded too evil to belong to her.

"I'll take you as well as him." A red glow flashed in her eyes. "I'll take all of you."

She glided forward like a wisp of smoke. Her body was ghostly, transparent, and floating several inches off the ground. I pointed my sword at the wraith, though the blade passed straight through her colorless form.

Her hand reached out and grasped my neck. A cold unlike anything I'd felt before pierced straight to my heart and froze me in place. My hands grew so stiff, I dropped the sword. It made a loud thump as it hit the forest floor.

I felt as if time stopped. I stood unarmed with the wraith's hands wrapping my neck, cutting off my breath, freezing the remaining air in my lungs. Everything was happening too fast. I was supposed to be saving my sister, but I was too late, and now she would kill me.

Tears stung my eyes as I looked into the wraith's face. I couldn't call her my sister anymore. There was nothing left of her, no spark in her eyes, no coy playfulness that I was so used to seeing. Nothing but milky white eyes that spoke of death.

"Ky..." I managed. "Stop. Please."

Spots danced in my vision, and it was then I knew my death was coming. No one had the power to stop a wraith—not even Fandalore, which was why the Wraith King had managed to survive all these thousands of years without dying.

My only comfort was knowing that if I died, at least I'd done it trying to save my sister.

A flash of purple light exploded around us. I fell back and hit the ground so hard, my teeth rattled in my skull. Still, I inhaled a deep breath and thanked the stars that I could breathe again.

A flock of cawing wing bodies swirled in a whirlwind around us. Their shrieks were deafening, although soon, they flew apart. My ears were left ringing, my neck bruised, and my heart shattered.

"What... what happened?" I asked as I sat up, rubbing the tender skin on my neck.

"Luria used her staff," Maharani explained. "She made the wraith... useless."

I glanced at Luria, who stood holding her staff and looking with an awestruck expression at the purple crystals glowing on top.

"Yes, very good," Fandalore exclaimed. "I told you that staff was useful."

Something flopped on the road in front of us, and I focused through still-blurry eyes on a crow with a broken wing attempting to fly. It held something in its beak, though I couldn't get a good look at it.

"Shoot it with your staff, Luria," Maharani urged.

"No, wait," I said, then climbed to my feet. Though I wobbled a bit, I managed to find my balance. "I don't think it's a threat."

Thimblethorn rustled his massive wings as he loomed behind us. "Take care," he said with a shudder. "Don't get close to it."

"But there's something in its beak," I said. My head felt fuzzy, my throat hurt, and a trickle of terror still dripped through my blood as I remembered the crazed look in the wraith's eyes. But since my sister had so recently been transformed into a flock of crows, perhaps this one remaining crow would give me some clue as to her current state—and how to reverse it.

I took another step forward and the thing in the crow's beak came into focus. I reached up and felt the tree pendant missing around my neck.

"It's got my pendant," I called over my shoulder to the others.

The crow hopped toward me, then placed the tree pendant on the ground at my feet. I knelt and took the pendant.

"Caw," the crow cried with a sound that sounded eerily like my sister when she screeched. "Caw-ree! Caw-ree!"

Maharani and Luria approached. Fandalore also drew nearer.

"Interesting," he mused, stroking the silver strands of his beard. "The staff seems to have transformed the wraith."

I cupped my hands and held them out to the crow, and it hopped onto my palms. It weighed so little I barely felt it. Intelligent eyes focused on me, and in their dark brown depths, I saw a spark of light. It looked nothing like the wraith, and so like Kyrie, I had to catch my breath.

"Are you... Kyrie?" I asked hesitantly.

"Caw-ree!" it agreed and flapped its good wing. It pecked at the tree pendant which I also held in my hand.

"You *are* Kyrie," I exclaimed.

"Your sister is a crow?" Maharani asked, disbelief in his voice.

"Yes. The staff of uselessness must have transformed her. Nice work, Luria."

She only shrugged. "I'm not even sure how I did it. I saw the wraith choking the life out of you, so I pointed my staff at it. Then, the staff sort of took over. I didn't even say any magic words or anything."

"Fueled by intense emotion, yes," Fandalore mused.

"Did you know it was fueled by emotion?" Luria challenged. "Because if so, then it was very rude of you not to tell me."

The old wizard frowned. "You forget my age, young Haemon. How is a wizard of so many years supposed to retain all the information gained after centuries? Eh?" He bounced on his toes, as if attempting to appear taller than his less than five feet. "You try cramming so many thoughts into one mind and see if you don't forget a thing or two?" He straightened out his blue robes. "Now. I should say this crow will be useful indeed. You, crow." He jabbed a finger at the bird's chest. "What information on the Wraith King can you tell us?"

I moved the crow away from the wizard's finger. "Her name isn't Crow," I said. "And I doubt she can speak."

"Then what should we call her?" Luria asked. "If this is really your sister, shouldn't we call her Kyrie?"

I thought about it for a moment until it hit me. "We'll call her Val. That's short for Valkyrie, which is Kyrie's full name. Valkyrie Dawn Simpleton. If we call her Val, we can distinguish her crow form from her human form."

"I like it," my cousin chimed in. "Valkyrie. Val. Makes sense."

The crow bobbed its head and cawed excitedly, and it wasn't hard to imagine Kyrie jumping up and down at the prospect of getting a "crow" name. She flapped her wings, although only one moved properly, and the other dragged.

"What will we do about this wing?" I asked.

"I don't know," Luria answered. "I guess when I used the spell, I must've injured her wing." She glanced at the crystals glowing on her staff. "I doubt this thing is any good at repairing or healing." She turned her gaze to Fandalore. "What about you? You're a wizard, right?"

"Yeah," Maharani agreed. "You're not just any wizard, either. You're *the* wizard. You're Fandalore."

"Well..." Fandalore placed his fists on his bony hips. "I may be a wizard, but I should warn you, I rarely interfere with problems you young pups should be solving yourselves. You can't expect me to come running every time and casting magic spells when you get into trouble. That being said, this bird's wing here can't be fixed without a good dose of magic, so, I shall make an exception."

"You'll heal her?" I asked expectantly.

"Yes. I may be an old fool, but if there's one thing I can't stand to see, it's a suffering creature. Now." He rolled up his sleeves. "Stand aside." Luria and Maharani moved back. He took a step toward the bird, then removed a wand from his robes. I'd never seen his wand until now. It was made of light-colored wood and was carved with ivy vines and berries all along its shaft. The strangest aspect of it was that I saw no place where the magical batteries would have been stored.

Fandalore waved his wand and mumbled a string of words I didn't understand. As he spoke, a gust of wind blew through the forest, and leaves tumbled in a torrent of golden-brown past us. The wind was warm and carried the scent of autumn. A shaft of sunlight broke through the clouds, somehow making it past all those thick tree branches and shone directly on the crow.

It was only now that I noticed the prism of colors—purples and greens—shining from its glossy feathers.

The crow stood so still, she could have been made of stone. She listened reverently to the wind. I detected the gentle sound of humming, as if someone were singing. It was a soft sound, but one that spoke directly to my soul. All my worries—that my sister was dying, that my dad was lost, that the Wraith King would soon take control of our world unless we stopped him—felt so far away. It was a fleeting moment, yet it gave me hope that perhaps one day, maybe I really could live without all those scary thoughts.

The song ended, and too soon, the sunlight faded. The crow bounced on my hand, then spread both her wings with the whooshing of feathers.

"Caw," she called as she took off.

"Well, she's better," Thimblethorn said with a twitch of his massive tail. "Let's just hope she comes back. Doesn't go and report our location to the Wraith King."

"I'm sure she won't," I said, watching as the black body grew smaller and smaller as it rose higher into the sky. Although I'd spoken with confidence, a seed of doubt lingered in the back of my mind. Kyrie would never report back to the Wraith King if she could help it, but what about Val? How much of Kyrie still existed inside the crow? Was there anything left of the wraith inside her?

"That was incredible magic," Luria addressed the wizard and spoke with awe in her voice. "You used a true song of Chorus to heal her?"

"Yes." Fandalore said with a wink to the Haemon girl. "The true magic of Chorus is rarely seen in our world anymore, not since those blasted magical factories have taken over. Still..." He stuck his wand back in his robes. "The magic of Chorus isn't gone for good, it's just a little harder to find."

"Should we keep going?" Maharani asked, glancing at the sky. "Or should we wait for Val to return?"

"Keep going," I answered. "She shouldn't have any trouble spotting us. I don't think so, anyway."

Evening approached as we wandered down one trail and then another. Although Maharani kept referring to his map, I could see the confusion written on his face as he looked from the branching paths in front of us, then back to the parchment scrawled with winding trails.

"Gordy," he finally confessed as we stood at another fork in the road. "I'm really sorry, cuz, but I think I'm lousy at this tracking thing. I think I've gotten us lost." Dejection filled his voice.

"Lost?" Luria questioned, her gaze darting to the overshadowing trees, as if they watched us. "In here?"

"Maybe we should set up camp," I offered, although I'd really been hoping we'd make it out of these woods before nightfall. I doubted I'd get any sleep in a creepy place like this.

"Yes," Fandalore said, pulling at his beard. "I'm afraid this young man is right. We'd be smart to make camp now before it gets any darker. A nice fire is in order, I'd say."

My shoulders slumped as I started gathering firewood with the others. A lingering fear trickled down my spine. Save for the one moment Fandalore had healed my sister's broken wing, I wasn't sure I'd felt at ease since entering the forest.

The worst feeling was sensing that the Wraith King could see us here. I kept looking over my shoulder, thinking another wraith would be near. It almost felt as if the Wraith King were toying with us. He'd sent my wraith sister to frighten us. In my brief interactions with him, I got the impression that he enjoyed seeing people afraid. I supposed as a wraith, any other emotions would be gone except terror.

Why couldn't the Wraith King see what a miserable existence that was? But Uncle Harlowe's words came back to me as I stacked another log on the wood pile. He'd reminded me that the Wraith King's mortal life had been filled with pain and misery. He'd never had the comforts I'd had—never even had a family who loved him. If I'd grown up with such a terrible life, wouldn't I have thought differently?

Maybe, I mumbled to myself. Except for never dying, I still couldn't see how becoming an undead wraith was preferable to living as a mortal.

"That should be good for now," Maharani said as he plopped the last log on the wood pile with a thunk that echoed through the forest.

I glanced back at our dragon, who'd curled up on the road and tucked his head under a wing. "Thimblethorn," I called. "It's your turn."

"Hmm?" He lazily raised his big head.

"Time to light the fire," I said, pointing to the wood pile.

"Very well," he said with a yawn, then opened his mouth and released a volley of white-gold flames that licked hungrily at the dry wood. Unlike last time, the fire didn't have any trouble spreading over the twigs and branches.

Soon, we sat around the fire and held our hands to the cheery orange flames. Fandalore managed to produce a handful of edible roots that he passed around to us. They were a far cry from the jerky, dried fruits, and thick rabbit stews adventurers had eaten on their journeys in my books. The roots were tough, and by the time I'd swallowed the tasteless, fibrous mass, my jaw ached from chewing so hard.

I rested my chin in my hands as I stared at the flames.

"Something the matter, young whip?" Fandalore asked. He spoke in an uncharacteristic gentle tone, reminding me of my grandfather. My hand went to my empty pocket where I'd so recently kept his watch.

"It's not like the books, is it?" I asked.

"Life is rarely like story books."

"Why?" I picked up a stick and tossed it into the fire, the scent of woodsmoke permeating the air. "Why can't life just be easy sometimes? Why does it always have to be so hard?"

"Do you want the comfortable answer?" he asked. "Or the genuine one?"

"Maybe I don't want an answer." I picked up another twig and broke it in half. If Grandpa had been here, he'd most likely have something encouraging to say. Tell me to focus on the positive. Look at that nice fire, he'd say. Your belly may be empty, but aren't you glad you have some heat on such a chilly evening?

As we settled to sleep under Thimblethorn's wing, a pang of home-sickness tugged at me so hard, I had to take a deep breath to keep the tears away. All I'd ever wanted was to leave home and have an adventure, and now all I wanted was to go back to the way things were.

Chapter 5
FORK IN THE ROAD

The sound of a mechanical buzz woke me. As I cracked my eyes open, I focused on a gray sky peeking behind the skeletal tree branches. It must have been just before dawn.

"What's that sound?" I mumbled to myself as I shifted beside my pack, and the buzzing increased until I recognized it. After reaching into my bag, I pulled out the scrying screen.

My heart leapt with excitement at the sight of the magical fog swirling around the oval-shaped screen. I hadn't spoken to Mom or Uncle Harlowe in ages. Could it be them calling me now?

"Maharani." I nudged my cousin's elbow, and he sat up with a start, his hair wild and eyes wide. "Look," I said. "I think our parents are calling."

"Oh." He rubbed his eyes. "Let's answer it."

"All right." I ran my finger over the screen's cold, concave glass, and the fog swirled before disappearing to reveal my mom and uncle.

"Mom," I gasped. "Uncle Harlowe!"

"Hi, sweetie." Mom's butterfly earrings jangled as she waved.

"Hey kiddos," Uncle Harlowe said in his deep voice. The familiarity of their voices made me feel like I'd been wrapped in a warm blanket, and I could almost imagine being home again.

"We were hoping we'd get through," Mom said. "They just restored the magical factory—well, partially, anyway. But it's working well enough to contact you." Her eyes shifted to Uncle, and I could see her desperation. "Gordy... I've got some very bad news. I don't know how to say this, but—"

"It's Kyrie," I said. "Yeah, I already know. She's been turned into a wraith."

"But..." Confusion clouded her gaze. "How?"

"Because she came to us in her wraith form. And, you won't believe this, but Luria managed to change her into a crow."

Mom looked dumbstruck and didn't speak for a moment. "A crow?"

"Yeah," Maharani answered. "We're calling her Val."

"But..." Mom blinked. "A crow?" she repeated.

"Yes, and she's okay, Mom," I said reassuringly. "I think if we can defeat the Wraith King, she'll be transformed back to her real self." That was a leap on my part. I had no idea if it was true, but I had to say something to reassure her. "Anyway, at least she's not a wraith anymore."

Mom only nodded and swallowed as tears sparkled in her eyes. Uncle Harlowe placed a big hand on her shoulder.

"We have more news," Uncle said. "Good and bad."

"Okay," I said, my gaze shifting to Maharani who had an equally concerned expression. "What's your news?"

"Good news first," Maharani said firmly.

"All right," Uncle agreed. "Good news first. We found your dad, Gordy."

"Really?" My heart gave such a giant leap, I was surprised it didn't burst out of my chest. "Where? How?"

"He was in the factory buried under a load of giant magical toad-stools."

My cousin wrinkled his forehead. "Uh, toadstools?"

"Yeah," I answered. "They grow them in farms, then transport them to the factories and use them as fuel for the generators. Don't you remember learning that in magical economics?"

"You know I never paid attention," he argued. "Anyway, is Gordy's dad okay?"

"Well... that's the bad news part. He's alive, and he's expected to make a full recovery, but for now, his skin is green, he's only speaking in croaks, and he's hopping."

I blinked. "Hopping?"

"Yes," Uncle answered. "Come to find out, those toadstools came from the Frogtopian Forest in the southern region and had a potent blend of transformation magic in their roots, which transferred to your father when he was buried under them. We're having to keep watch on him day and night. He keeps escaping out to the pond and trying to eat flies while he sits on lily pads. It's problematic considering he weighs a hundred times that of a common bullfrog. Hardly the body type to be balancing on lily pads."

"We've had to pull him out of the pond twice now," Mom said. "Soaking wet and croaking his poor green head off."

"Oh," was all I could manage as I imagined the ridiculous sight.

"We're making do," Mom said. "We put him in the bathtub, and he seems content enough."

"Unfortunately," my uncle continued. "We're in lockdown here in Kroy Wen. Mayor Wren issued stay-at-home orders for everyone in the city. With so many people getting transformed into wraiths, she doesn't want anyone venturing outdoors, and my whole unit is in an uproar trying to enforce it. I'd planned to come out and help you as soon as I could, but now..."

"It's all right, Dad," Maharani said. "We're doing okay."

"You're sure?" Mom asked.

"Positive," I answered, not bothering to mention how I'd nearly been choked to death by my wraith sister.

"You're probably safer there anyway," Mom said, dabbing at the corner of her eye with a tissue. "The wraiths have descended on the city. They're determined to transform every last person into one of them. Thankfully, we've put charms on our doors and windows to repel them—as have most people. It's giving the wraiths trouble for sure."

Behind us, Luria had sat up. She must've been listening for some time when she spoke up. "What about the bomb to destroy the Dragon Wraith Mountains—to destroy my people?" She spoke with heat in her voice. "Are they still bent on going through with it?"

"No," Uncle said, and Luria gave an audible sigh of relief. "President Falcoon stepped in and talked Mayor Wren out of using any bombs. They're taking another approach now, although they're tightlipped on what it is."

"Alexander Bravestone," I said without hesitation. "It's gotta be."

"Bravestone, yes," Uncle stroked the blond strands of his beard. "I've heard of him. The Chosen Hero, huh?"

"It's ridiculous," I said.

"It may be ridiculous, but it's giving people something to talk about. I wouldn't use the word *hope* quite yet, although I'm sure that's the intention."

"He's a total actor," my cousin said. "You can look at him and see he's a fake."

"If you must know—and I'm telling you this in confidence—it wasn't Mayor Wren's idea to use him. This comes straight from President Falcoon. He hired a team to create the Chosen Hero distraction."

"I knew it," Luria hissed, showing her short, pointed fangs, as she shook her head.

"That's so stupid," I said. "*We* were the ones who had the idea first. Not him. And we've even got the true Hero's sword and the real wizard Fandalore. Why aren't we on all those news programs and stuff?"

"Gordy," Uncle said in his gentle, fatherly tone. "This may be hard to believe, but you're in a better position than Alexander Bravestone. Press coverage for someone like him can be a very dangerous thing."

"What do you mean?" my cousin asked.

"What do you think would happen if the Wraith King really did take this kid seriously?" Uncle answered. "Or even if the Wraith King doesn't take him seriously, what if he decides to make a spectacle of this kid calling himself the Chosen Hero?"

I thought about what Uncle was implying. "I guess if the Wraith King wanted, he could destroy Bravestone just like he did all those other would-be Chosen, wait for a time when Bravestone was on TV or something to do it. It would be a good way to crush people's spirits."

"Exactly," Uncle said. "Making Bravestone such a visible target isn't a wise decision, in my opinion, although I doubt the Wraith King wants to waste any resources on this kid just yet."

"I guess," I answered, although a drop of jealousy still sparked inside me anytime someone said the name Alexander Bravestone. The others told Uncle about how we were heading to the Knight's training facility, and how we hoped to use our new weapons before journeying off to the Dragon Wraith Mountains to confront the Wraith King. We still hadn't come up with a solid plan of attack, although we had two things working in our favor: we had Luria to get us through the maze of the Dragon Wraith Mountains, and we had the Hero's sword.

Having it meant I had no choice but to confront the Wraith King, even though terror like nothing I'd ever experienced froze me when I thought about it. For one thing, my own grandfather said I wouldn't be able to kill the Wraith King. And there was something else, something that bothered me just as much. It was a conversation I'd had with Luria. I'd been having nightmares about seeing a shadow being called a mythriwraith. It looked just like the Wraith King except in spirit form. She'd told me that anyone who saw one was destined to be killed by the Wraith King. She'd laughed it off and called it an old superstition, yet why did it ring with such truth to me?

By the time we ended the call with my mom and Uncle Harlowe, the sky had lightened to a shade of dusky pink. We packed up what little we had and continued down the trail. Tree branches stretched like skeletal arms over our path.

Talking to my mom and uncle had eased my tension, but only for a moment. Now, I found myself dragging my feet again. I couldn't seem to shake the feeling of dread that had been chasing me since the moment we'd stepped into the forest.

"Which way?" Luria asked as we got to a fork in the road.

"Umm..." Maharani said. "See, that's a problem. I sort of lost track of where we are."

"So." Luria placed her hands on her hips. "We're lost?"

"Pretty much." Maharani kicked a rock with the toe of his shoe.

"And our wizard is gone again," Luria said with a sigh. "Conveniently. When we need him."

"Yeah," I agreed. What if Fandalore was wandering away on purpose? Maybe this was a test or something, to see if we could manage without him. So far, it seemed like we were failing spectacularly.

Thimblethorn blew steam from his nostrils. "Don't look at me," he said. "I'm afraid I haven't eaten a decent meal in a day and a half. My blood sugar's is far too low for me to be making decisions of any importance."

"I'm really sorry," my cousin said. "I guess I'm lousy at this tracker stuff."

I went to Maharani and placed a hand on his shoulder. "Anybody would get lost in a place like this," I said. "I mean, look at it. It's a labyrinth in here."

"Then what are we supposed to do?" Maharani asked. "We can't just wander around in here forever."

"Ugh." Luria shuddered and ran her hands over her arms. "That would be horrible."

Above us, a crow cawed.

"Is that...?" my cousin started to say when the crow descended toward us.

"Yeah," I answered. "I think it's Val."

The crow circled lower, and I held out my hand. Feathers ruffled as the crow landed on my arm with a loud *caw*. Then she shifted and dropped something in my palm.

"What's that?" Luria stepped closer and peered at the object in my hand. It was a small gray pebble.

"It's just a rock," Maharani said. "Why'd she bring that?"

"I don't know." I picked up the rock with my free hand and inspected it. It had a rectangular shape on two sides, as if it had been carved, although the rest of the stone had rough edges, like it had fallen off a bigger piece.

I bounced it in my hand as I pondered its significance. "This looks like it came from a bigger, shaped stone. Like something you'd find on a castle."

"Maybe the Knight's castle?" Maharani asked.

"Yes," I answered. "Possibly."

Maharani grinned and bounced on his toes. "She's saved us," he exclaimed. "Val, can you guide us to the castle?"

Val squawked with a sound that reminded me of Kyrie's, then she leapt off my arm and flew into the air, circled above us, and headed out of sight.

"Umm..." my cousin said. "Where'd she go? How are we supposed to follow her when we can't see her?"

"I think I can be of use." Thimblethorn stretched his neck to its full length until his head rose above the treetops, and I was reminded of what an enormous creature he was. "Indeed. I see her. To the northwest," he called.

"This path." My cousin pointed to the path branching to the left, and we took it without hesitation, walking more quickly than we had at any other time. Walking at a swift pace felt odd, making me realize that I'd mostly been dragging myself along the whole time we'd been here. It also made me realize how gloomy this place was, and how disheartened I'd felt, as if the hulking trees were instead the imposing walls of a dungeon.

At each branching path, Thimblethorn called out the direction Val was flying, and Maharani led us down one trail and then another, until we finally reached the edge of the forest. Sunlight bathed us as we walked out of the dark forest. I took a deep breath, feeling as if I could finally breathe again.

"We made it," I said with a long exhale. "Can you believe it?"

We stood on a small hill overlooking a valley. A carpet of vibrant green grass blew in the wind like waves on an ocean. At the bottom of the valley sat a castle with a red flag fluttering from its tallest tower.

"The Scared Knight's Castle," I said excitedly. "That's got to be it!"

"Let's go!" Maharani said, pumping his fist in the air. "Now Gordy can finally get trained, and me and Luria can practice using our weapons. We can all learn how to defeat the Wraith King, and Thimblethorn can finally have a decent meal so his low blood sugar won't kill him."

With that, we set off down the hill and toward the castle. It sat alone in a sea of green grass, without a village or any other buildings around it. The whole place buzzed with the feeling of magic, similar to what I'd felt when Fandalore had used the spell to fix Val's wing. It made me wonder what kind of place this was. Without a village or anything surrounding it to bring in crops, it must have run strictly on magic.

The closer we got to the castle, the more my stomach twisted with nervousness. What kind of place was this? What if the people inside were reclusive or hostile? We didn't know anything about the knights except what Fandalore had told us—that they were either scared or scarred or both—and now the wizard was missing once again. He wasn't even around to introduce us.

We spotted a cobbled trail leading to the castle gates. The worn stones were cracked, and weeds grew so thickly, it was hard to spot the path in places. We approached the base of the broad oaken gates which spanned up several stories. Only the flapping flag made any sound as the fabric got tugged in the breeze.

"Do we knock?" Luria asked.

"I guess." I reached up and grabbed a big bronze loop, then banged it three times on the door.

A cloud of blue fog emanated from the doors just before it swung open to reveal an empty courtyard. A shiver raced down my spine, as if warning me not to go inside.

But my cousin and Luria strode past me, so I suppressed my fear, then took my first step inside the Scared Knight's Castle.

Chapter 6

THE SCARED KNIGHT'S CASTLE

"Hello?" I called, my voice echoing through the empty courtyard. The paving stones were broken just like the ones on the path leading here, and weeds peeked from the ground. A few smaller buildings built of crumbling stones filled the courtyard, and beyond those was a large, towering structure that must've been the castle proper.

"No one here to greet us?" Thimblethorn asked, scratching his scaled chin with a claw. "How odd."

I heaved a frustrated sigh. "It would be nice if Fandalore were here to point us in the right direction—or at least tell us if we're even in the right place."

We crossed toward one of the smaller buildings. Decorating the top of the building was a weathervane in the shape of a Treble clef combined with a Bass clef to form the shape of a heart.

Luria pointed at it. "Look at that. That's a temple from ancient times, when Chaos and Chorus were represented as equal parts of a whole."

"I've never seen a symbol like that before," I mused. "It's really strange."

"It's not strange to me," Luria said. "I grew up on stories of how Chorus and Chaos were brothers who were only able to exist because of the other."

"But Chaos is evil," Maharani said. "He shouldn't exist at all."

"He's not evil." Luria spoke with a condescending tone. "Yes, certain followers of Chaos—namely the Wraith King—made him into a being more powerful than the original stories. They twisted his meaning and made him into something wicked, which is most likely why your people think he's so bad. But if you read the Book of Chaos, you'd know that Chorus can only exist because of Chaos, and vice versa. They're two halves of a whole."

"Well," my cousin said with a shrug. "You'll never get me to believe in Chaos."

I cast him a sidelong glance. "This coming from the kid who recently stole the Book of Chaos to find out more about the Haemon people?"

"Yeah..." he hedged, running a hand through his poofy curls. "But I only did that because I was curious about where I came from, you know? What my people believed in and stuff. I didn't actually intend on worshipping Chaos or anything. Don't they perform human sacrifices? I mean, that's not just ultra-gross, it's super evil."

"Not all his worshippers do human sacrifices." Luria continued with her condescending tone. "That's a very small group you're talking about. Most worshippers of Chaos abhor that kind of thing."

We continued toward the ancient relic of a temple when my toe snagged on something hidden in the weeds, nearly making me trip.

"What was that?" I looked down to see a bleached white bone—a leg bone, maybe? As I studied the weed-choked ground, I noticed more bones peeking from the grass. In one corner, I spotted a human skull. "Umm..." I said hesitantly.

"See what I mean?" my cousin said in a shaky voice, his face going pale. "Human sacrifices. I told you so. We should get out of here, and fast."

"Nay," a booming voice announced. "Those are the bones of our enemies, and you tread on sacred ground."

A tall, cloaked figure emerged from the castle door.

"Who—who are you?" Maharani choked.

The man strode closer. His silver eyes matched his hair and silky-smooth beard that fell to his chest. There was something odd about him, as if he weren't quite human. Maybe it was the silvery sheen glowing from his eyes, as if they were lit with moonlight, or maybe it was his height, which would have dwarfed Uncle Harlowe if he'd been here.

"I am a member of the Sacred Knights of Evalon, member of the knights of the Eight Tables, and you are trespassing on holy ground." He spoke with a forceful tone.

"Sac-red," Maharani said quietly, almost under his breath. "I knew it couldn't have been Scared."

"Or Scarred," I added in a whisper.

"What is your business here?" the man demanded. "Tell me now before I am forced to dispatch you."

"*Dispatch* us?" Maharani mumbled to me with a fearful glance. "That's a fancy word for kill, you know."

"Yeah, I know," I whispered back.

The man took another step forward, his presence overbearing, and I had no doubt he meant to go through with *dispatching* us should he find us unworthy.

"Wait," I said, holding up my hands. "We're not enemies, and we're not here to cause trouble. We were told you could train us how to use our weapons."

"Weapons?" He eyed me. "You've brought weapons *here*?" he demanded. "To holy grounds?"

My heart pounded. "I—we—" I cast a pleading glance at my friends, although they looked as stunned as me. Something had gone horribly wrong. We must have been at the incorrect castle, and this man was about to kill us for bringing weapons on sacred ground.

"What weapons do you have?" he demanded.

I unsheathed the sword from the leather scabbard hanging on my left hip. "Yo-ho," it called in a sing-song voice. "Finally found it within you to unsheathe me, have you? I'll have you know, I'm not used to being kept in the dark for such a long period of time, you ungracious, ill-mannered—"

"Sorry," I mumbled to the man, then stuffed Schubert back into the scabbard. "Wrong sword."

The man arched an eyebrow in an exaggerated gesture. I grabbed the pommel from the sheath on my opposite side and pulled out the real sword. I really needed to wrap a cord around Schubert's hilt or something so I could tell the two apart.

Stupid Schubert was going to get me killed.

"Is that...?" the man started, then strode forward with eyes narrowed.

"It's the Hero's sword," I said.

"Where in all of Alderfell did you get that?" he asked in a hushed tone.

"From the dungeons under the Elderhurst ruins," I answered.

"Well then." He ran a finger through the strands of his beard. "This changes things, doesn't it?" He clapped a hand on my shoulder, and his scowl turned to a grin that brightened his whole face. "Welcome to the Sacred Knight's Castle, young hero. We've been expecting you." He nodded to my friends and to Thimblethorn who stood behind us. "And welcome to your friends as well. Let the training begin."

Chapter 7

THE HALL OF EIGHT TABLES

"I can't believe we made it inside," my cousin said in a rushed whisper as we paced through a giant doorway to enter the castle proper. "I thought we were dead."

"I know," I answered as we followed the tall man. We'd left Thimblethorn in the courtyard, and the man had assured us our dragon would be well-cared for—and most importantly, he would be fed. I'd never seen such a gleeful dragon.

Now, we followed the man into a circular room. It must have been part of an enormous tower. Above us, the ceiling rose at least ninety feet into the air. Sunlight shone inside through the numerous keyhole shaped windows ringing the walls all the way from top to bottom. The light painted the flagstone floor in a pattern like a patchwork quilt.

Statues as tall as three men stood around the room's perimeter. The marble was carved to be so lifelike I could almost feel their eyes watching me as we crossed to the room's center. The most unusual aspect of the space was the numerous tables in various stages of disrepair. They were all shaped oddly—some as octagons, others as triangles or pentagons. Some were missing legs; others were broken in half.

"What's with all these weird tables?" Luria whispered to us.

"No idea," I answered. "It's strange, though."

After passing through the tower room, we entered a hallway. Laughter came from up ahead. We entered a small chamber. A fire crackled from a fireplace so large, it took up the entire back wall. A layer of soot clung to the surrounding carved marble, making it appear black in places. A rug woven from scraps of old rags covered the flagstone floor, and overstuffed couches and chairs had been placed in a semicircle around the hearth.

Two older gentlemen sat talking on the couches facing away from us. Although I could only see the backs of their heads from this angle, I would recognize that wheezy laughter anywhere.

When I stepped to the front of the couch and faced the two men, my suspicions were confirmed. "Fandalore." I placed my hands on my hips.

"What are you doing here?" Luria demanded, her voice edged with exasperation.

"You got here *before* we did?" Maharani chimed in. "Where were you? Why weren't you with us when that tall guy nearly killed us?"

"Don't you listen to anything?" he challenged. "A wizard can't be expected to pull you out of every sticky situation. Besides." He waved his hand. "I knew you would make it here safely."

"You could have at least waited for us," Luria demanded.

"What do you think I've been doing?" he asked with a wry chuckle. "Now, let's not quibble over things in the past that no one can change." He cleared his throat. "Let me introduce you to the only two remaining knights of Evalon." He motioned to the man sitting beside him and the tall man who stood behind us. "Meet Sir John Johnson." He pointed to the man behind us. "And Sir Donald Donaldson." He motioned to the man sitting beside him.

My friends and I traded confused glances. "Um... John and Donald?" I asked.

"That's right," the wizard answered with a vigorous nod. "Sirs John Johnson and Donald Donaldson are the last two knights of Evalon, although there were eight to begin with. Apparently, Sirs Eric Ericson, William Williamson, Bran Branson, Jack Jackson, Peter Peterson, and Richard Richardson have all completed their quests and earned their places in the Hall of Eight Tables."

"That is correct," the man sitting beside Fandalore—Sir Donald—said. I hadn't gotten a good look at him until now. He looked like his companion, John, although his hair was the golden color of flax and not silver. He wore his beard in the same style, long and neatly combed. His eyes held a golden glow, just as his companion's had a silvery glow.

Although the golden glow of his eyes held an otherworldly, almost angelic appearance, his clothing choices destroyed the impression. He wore mismatched robes in a patchwork of clashing colors.

"Eh," my cousin said and cleared his throat. "Why do all the knights have such funny names?"

"It just happened that way," Donald said with a chuckle. "Odd coincidence. Funny how those coincidences happen. Maybe we could learn something from that sort of thing."

"We'll have to learn something soon, won't we, Don?" Sir John said with a severe frown, and I detected a hint of displeasure in his voice.

Sir Donald waved his hand. "I'm in no hurry."

"Yes," Sir John answered darkly. "I've noticed."

"How good are you at training?" Luria cut in, hands on her hips. "We've come a long way, and we'd like to get started soon, if you please."

"All in good time," Fandalore said. "First, we shall allow these good knights to take us to their tower and show us these mysterious tables they've been going on about. Fascinating conundrum."

The three men led us out of the room, back through the hallway we'd come from, and into the tower with the broken tables.

"It's an impossible situation," Donald said, shaking his head as he looked with frustration at the tables littering the room.

"What is?" Maharani asked.

"Ah, such a shame," Sir John added. "You see, when the knights first organized more than a thousand years ago, there were eight of us. Thus, an eight-sided table was in order." He led us to a large, octagonal-shaped table covered in a dusty cloth. "Eight sides, you see. For eight knights."

"Yes," Sir Donald added. "Sir Richard was the first to complete his life's quest and be entombed in his statue in the Hall of Eight Tables." He pointed up to one of the enormous statues. "Sirs Peter, Jack, and Bran came next. Putting us down to four knights remaining. An uncomplicated square-shaped table. Those were memorable days," he said with a faraway look.

"Ah, yes," Sir John said with a hint of nostalgia in his voice. "Lovely times. Simple days. Just the four of us at a plain, uncomplicated square table, discussing our plans, how to improve our lives and better others in the process. Of course, those days couldn't last. They never do. Sir William achieved his life's mission first. He found out how to love unselfishly, not an easy task for him, may Chorus bless his soul. That left three of us." He pointed to a triangular table, and we walked to it.

"We could see it coming, of course," Sir Donald said, rapping his knuckles on the tabletop. "We knew the day would come that one of us would complete our life's mission. We didn't expect it to be Sir Eric. He'd always had such trouble with jealousy, you see. We thought he would be the last. But no, he had an epiphany on one of his quests. He was tasked with helping a spoiled young prince to realize his blessings. He went on to apply those same principles to his own life. He understood how jealousy had no place in it. And so, he earned his place in his statue." He pointed up to one of the looming stone figures.

"Which leaves us here," Sir John said with a sigh. "Two of us remaining, and no table that can possibly suit our situation. There are no such things as two-sided tables." He pounded his fist on the table as he said it. "You might suggest a circle, of course. A circle can fit a dozen people or more depending on the table's size. Yes, of course it can. But the circle is the most sacred symbol of all, reserved for either Sir Donald or me. The final table. But the table we need now is most impossible."

"A table with only two sides?" Fandalore questioned. "Yes, I can see the problem."

"You can't imagine how many hours we've lain awake at night pondering our situation."

"Geometrically impossible," Sir Donald added in a forlorn voice that spoke of untold frustration. "We've torn down all the old tables and reconstructed them time and time again, hoping to get some clue as to how to build a new one. But it's no use." His shoulders sagged.

I stood by my cousin and Luria as the knights continued moaning about their table-less situation. Luria's gaze went up to the towering statues, and it was only now I realized that six of them held a faint bluish glow.

"This is such a ridiculous place." Luria spoke quietly so the knights couldn't hear.

"Do you really think they'll know how to train you, Gordy?" my cousin asked.

"Yes," I answered. "I mean, Fandalore made us come here for a reason. He said they were the best, didn't he?"

"Oh, I don't doubt they can train you," Luria said. "If they'll ever shut up about that table."

The knights moaned for another half hour. My friends and I had found seats at the five-sided table while we waited, until finally the three men crossed toward us.

"...which leads us to the training of this young whelp." Fandalore strode toward us, and the two knights followed. "He's a decent youth, not too spoiled from what I can see, which is a positive for him. Still..." Fandalore tugged at his beard. "He needs training if he's to battle the Wraith King. And even more training if he wishes to defeat him."

"We've trained many a young squire," Donald announced confidently. "You, young man, tell us your name again?"

"Gordy Simpleton," I answered.

He frowned, as if displeased.

"Or Tevyn." I stood taller. "Tevyn Brightblade. At least... that's my hero's name."

"But you feel more comfortable being called by your given name?"

"Yeah." I chanced a glance at my friends. "I guess I was excited at first to have a real hero's name, but somehow, I feel more comfortable being called Gordy. Just Gordy." I shrugged. I wasn't sure I was making a great impression on the knight, although I did think it best to be honest with him.

"Well then, if that is your wish, you shall go by Gordy here at our castle. What you choose to be called outside our castle is another matter."

Sir John clapped his hands. "We shall start your training immediately. Come, I shall escort you to our weaponry."

"Wait." I held up my hand, stopping him. "My friends are here for training as well. My cousin Maharani has a shield, and my friend Luria needs help with her magical staff. Any assistance you could give them would be appreciated."

"Very well," Sir John said with a polite nod. "You three youths shall all be trained. Come. You have much to learn."

Chapter 8
THE CHOSEN HERO

If I could sum up my training in one word, it would have to be brutal. By the time afternoon arrived, my muscles had turned to lead weights, and I couldn't move without audibly wincing. Maharani and Luria weren't faring much better, although Luria did seem to be gaining more control over the staff of uselessness, and Maharani had learned several cool maneuvers with his shield.

"I thought you said I had fifteen minutes," I said to Sir Donald as he stood over me, sword in hand. The man hadn't broken a sweat the entire time we'd trained, which I guess made sense, since I suspected he was half immortal. He was how many hundreds of years old?

"It's been long enough for you to regain your breath. Come, you have much to learn still."

I wanted to argue and tell him I wasn't sure I would be able to stand up, much less hold my sword, but then I imagined the Wraith King challenging me. He wouldn't be giving me any breaks if I really had to fight him.

I still hadn't come to terms with the idea of battling the Wraith King. For so long, I'd imagined being a pretend Chosen One. A distraction. I couldn't possibly battle him myself. But the sword had changed all that. And although my grandfather's words rang in my head... *you're not the Chosen One. You can never be...* I still went along with the training. Maybe I could prove to my grandfather that I really could be more than he thought.

"Hold your ground," Sir Donald instructed. "Don't let me control the direction. It only takes one good hit to end a match."

His training hadn't been what I'd thought. For one, our matches only lasted a few seconds until he bested me. I'd hoped to at least go for a minute or two before being disarmed. He hadn't shown mercy. Hadn't relented. Although he'd only pretended to stab me through my heart or slit my throat, I still felt wholly defeated by the end of the day.

Maharani, Luria, and I marched into the courtyard as evening fell. Thimblethorn lay outside on a giant bed of straw. He picked the meat from a pile of chicken bones and smacked his lips.

Exhausted, we collapsed onto the straw beside him.

"I'm dead," Maharani wailed. "I've never felt so bone weary in my whole life."

"Yeah," I groaned with him. "Every muscle in my body is aching. Even my pinkie finger is sore!"

Luria only shook her head at us.

"What?" I demanded. "Aren't you tired, too? You trained just as hard as us, right?"

She placed her staff across her lap. "I was training with magical spells. Mental stuff mostly."

I rubbed my neck. Cawing rang out, and a feathery black body descended from the sky, then landed beside me. I patted the crow's head, and she gave me a once-over, as if to ask if I was okay.

"Hi, Val," I said. "Yes, I'm fine. Training to defeat the Wraith King is no joke."

She cawed again, as if to tell me something. Or warn me of something.

Maharani sat up, then stared overhead at the darkening sky. "Does anyone hear that?"

"Hear what?" I asked, just before the sound of droning engines emanated from above.

Lights shone in the sky, growing brighter, and I could make out the shapes of mechanical Pegasi and drago-drones descending on us.

"What's going on?" my cousin questioned.

"I don't know," I answered as the lights continued growing brighter, until I had to shield my eyes as they dropped into the courtyard.

A lightweight, blue-scaled dragon landed first, followed by a collection of Pegasi hitched to coaches, and drago-drones buzzing around them. On the sides of the coaches, in glossy black letters, were the words ALEXANDER BRAVESTONE-CHOSEN HERO.

"Oh. My. Chaos," Luria bit out. "You *can't* be serious."

The blue dragon snorted as one of the coach's doors opened. A man with shiny polished shoes strode out of a vehicle. He wore a business suit, glasses without rims, and had hair so dark and so slick with gel, it could have been made of wrought iron. If I'd knocked on his head, I had the feeling I'd hear it clanging.

He glanced at us briefly with narrowed eyes, although his gaze mainly focused on Thimblethorn. His face was all angles and sharp features. There wasn't anything soft about him.

He pressed a hand to his ear where he must have been wearing some kind of magical listening device. Communicating with someone, maybe?

"Safe," was all I heard when another of the coach's doors opened. Alexander Bravestone climbed out.

He wasn't as tall as he'd looked in the interviews, though still taller than me. With his sour frown and hands stuck in his pockets, he also didn't look nearly so cheerful—or so giddy to go and defeat the Wraith King as he'd been on the magi-box interview.

"Who are you?" he called in a demanding voice after he'd taken a few steps out of the carriage.

"I—umm... we're..." I tried speaking. I really did. But what was I supposed to say to a kid with a reputation like his?

"We're here for training," Luria said. "Yes, before you ask. I'm Haemon. And these are my friends." She pointed at me. "This is Gordy Simpleton." She shifted to point at my cousin. "And this is Maharani Swordsong. I'm called Luria." She held out her hand.

Alexander's eyes narrowed at Luria's hand. He seemed focused on the red-and-black scales covering her skin. "Haemon, are you?" His lips twisted, as if he'd just eaten a lemon, and he kept his hands in his pockets without shaking her hand.

"What about you?" My cousin spoke up. "Why are you here?"

"Also training." He gave us a narrow-eyed gaze before the man with the shiny hair approached us.

"Bravestone," he called brusquely. "Inside." He thrust a thumb over his shoulder. "Now."

"Fine," he said with a sing-song sigh, rolled his eyes, and turned away from us. We all stood in slack-jawed silence as Bravestone and the man disappeared inside the castle. Behind them walked a group of ten or so people. Their shirts read SECURITY. After they strode inside came another group of at least a dozen people. Some carried cameras, others lugged heavy-looking garment bags. Some pushed carts carrying theater lights or makeup bags. Another rolling cart had weapons piled on it. What a circus.

"He's training?" I blurted.

"I'm not surprised," Luria said with a shake of her head. "The interview hinted he was up to something. The next logical step after securing a dragon, wizard, and a sword, are to start training."

"But he doesn't have any of those things," I argued. "At least, not any of the right things."

"Doesn't matter," my cousin said with a shrug of his big shoulders. "It's the appearance that counts. How he looks when cameras are rolling, you know."

"Yeah," I answered. "Right."

"By Chaos." Luria threw her hands in the air. "This is awful timing. Why is he here at the same time as us? Of all the stupid coincidences."

I tiled my head. "Well... Sir John—or was it Donald—did tell us to be mindful of coincidences."

The blue dragon—Opalesque dragon, maybe? —had remained outside with a few handlers, who promptly gave her a bag of apples and starting oiling her scales with cloths. I worried Thimblethorn might be jealous of the attention the dragon was getting, but he only propped his head on his tail and yawned.

Glancing at the big oak doors leading inside the castle, I couldn't push the image of Alexander Bravestone out of my head. His name was all over those stupid coaches, too. He was taller than me and had a sturdier, more muscular frame. His blond hair wasn't all messed up like mine always was, and he had been very charming on camera. I could see why President Falcoon thought he'd make a good Chosen Hero.

I clenched my fist around the pommel of my sword that I wore at my waist. *But he doesn't have this...* I reminded myself.

"Should we get inside?" my cousin asked. "See how the training is going?"

"Or *if* it's going," Luria said darkly. "Maybe the knights will refuse to train him."

I smiled inwardly. "Now that, I'd like to see."

Chapter 9

INTRODUCING MR. CASH MONEYMAKER, HANDLER AT LARGE

"**I** refuse." Alexander Bravestone seethed as he stood across from the shiny-haired man.

"You can't refuse, Al," the man snapped back. "You don't have that authority. I'm your handler. Have been since you signed the paperwork, remember? You said you wanted fame. This is how you get it."

Alexander's eyes simmered with unrestrained hatred. "Fine," he bit out. "But I'll only train while the cameras are rolling, and not a moment longer."

"Good enough," the man said, giving the boy a gloating smile before turning and snapping at two camera operators who stood in the corner. "You two," he called. "Start rolling as soon as Al is in wardrobe."

My friends and I stood in the Hall of Eight Tables watching the spectacle play out. I wasn't sure whether to laugh or to grimace. Seeing Alexander Bravestone in person certainly hadn't played out how I'd expected. I'd assumed he'd be extra peppy, smiling all the time, throwing out memorable quotes about how he'd soon put an end to the

Wraith King. Instead, he stood with crossed arms and distrustful eyes, giving off an air of blatant defiance.

The shiny-haired man waltzed toward me and my friends. "We'll have to clear out this area," he shouted over his shoulder to a camera operator. "You three," he called to me and my friends, then snapped his fingers. "Back away. We need this area for the cameras." He called over his shoulder again. "Can we get some of these tables cleared out as well? There's no room to move around."

"Sorry," Maharani said, clearing his throat. "Who are you? Because we were sort of here first."

He gave us a shrewd glance. "Cash Moneymaker," he snapped. "Handler of Alexander Bravestone." He tilted his head. "Why are you children here?" he demanded. "Shouldn't you be in school? Where are your parents?"

"I'm training," I spoke up. "To be the Chosen One."

"Chosen One?" He gave a derisive laugh. "You're joking."

"No," Luria snapped impatiently. "We're dead serious, and Gordy is ten times more Chosen than the actor you've brought along with you."

"Ah." Mr. Moneymaker rubbed his chin and glanced behind him. "Actor, yes. Funny you mention that. Alexander is a great stage actor. Won an award for his part in Midsummer Knight's Dream. You umm... saw Al's attitude just then, did you?" He shook his head. "I wish he'd be more tactful off camera. Thinks the only time he has to be in character is when the magi-tape is rolling." He gave me another glance. "So, you're on the same path as Al, are you? Who's your handler?"

"Handler?" I raised my eyebrows.

"Yes, your agent. You do have an agent, don't you?"

"Umm... not really."

He frowned, and his brows furrowed deeply, making him look older. "Don't have an agent? Then what are you doing here at this castle without adult supervision? How old are you?"

"Thirteen," I answered. "But that's not the point. I'm here because I'm training to *actually* defeat the Wraith King. Not pretend."

"Really?" He gave another mocking chuckle. "At thirteen, no less?"

"It's around the same age as all the other Chosen," my cousin argued. "Plus, Gordy's got a dragon, the real wizard Fandalore, and even the true Hero's sword."

Mr. Moneymaker frowned. "Not possible. Fandalore is dead. Has been for hundreds of years. And that sword is lost."

"It's the real one all right," Maharani rebutted with an edge of heat in his voice. "Gordy got it from the Elderhurst ruins and everything. Had to trade his grandpa's watch for it. Even saw the shadow of the Wraith King after he took it, so we know it's the real one."

"Shadow of the Wraith King, huh?" He chuckled.

"Yes," Maharani said defensively. "Gordy." He elbowed me. "Show him."

"I'm not so sure, cuz," I said under my breath.

"Yes, show him," he insisted.

"All right," I said, awkwardly reaching for the sword on my left hip, and thankfully removing the non-talking weapon.

Mr. Moneymaker gave it a cursory glance, eyebrows knit in concentration, then held his hand above it. "Hmm..." he mumbled, then pulled a wand from his suit jacket's pocket. He tapped the sword twice, and a faint blue glow, like the glow surrounding the knight's statues, came from the blade. "Interesting piece," he said offhandedly, then stuck the wand back in his pocket. "But unfortunately, totally worthless. Any lookalike sword will do in a situation like ours, preferably one that reflects the light well on camera. You might think this blade has some kind of great power. It doesn't. Great history, though. You might get a few coins for it from a museum."

I sheathed my sword, fuming. The nerve of this guy! I was tempted to pull out Schubert just for the opportunity of hearing the weapon chew out Mr. Moneymaker for calling all lookalike swords the same. He'd get an earful for sure. But Mr. Moneymaker spun around and gave us a dismissive wave. "You children clear out. I'm not in the habit of asking twice."

A gaggle of camera operators scooted beside us, and chiming voices rang out as Alexander Bravestone reappeared in the room. He'd cleaned up, had his hair brushed in silky waves that fell to his shoulders, and wore hero's garb, including an expensive-looking red cloak and polished leather boots.

"Oh, please," Luria grumbled under her breath. "Let's get out of here. We're done with training for today anyway."

Voices called out for Alexander to pose with his sword raised, pose with it pointed at the camera, pose smiling, pose with Sir John, pose with grim determination. I tried not to gag as I walked with my friends out of the training room. We found Fandalore napping on a couch. I debated on waking him, asking what he thought of the pretend Chosen Hero, but decided against it. Fandalore hadn't been much help on this trip. I doubted he'd be much help now.

Sir Donald met us in the hallway. "Wandering the castle, I see. Would you like me escort you somewhere?"

"Anywhere as far away from Alexander Bravestone as we can get," Luria said curtly.

"Ah, of course. Not fond of the young hero, are you?"

"He's no hero," my cousin said. "He's just about as much a hero as Schubert claims to be."

We giggled at that, and the golden-haired knight led us down a hallway and to a broad stone staircase. Suits of armor stood on each side, and a chandelier made of deer antlers hung overhead. After hiking up the stairs, we made it up several more flights until we arrived at a room in a tower.

Eight beds covered in dark burgundy comforters ringed the walls. Their bedframes were carved with cherubs and had ornate pillars that held rails with curtains in the same deep wine color.

"Will this suit your needs?" Sir Donald asked.

"Perfect." My cousin plopped his shield by the nearest bed, then jumped onto the mattress that squeaked under his weight.

"Ah yes," Sir Donald said. "The first bedchamber of the Eight Knights. We all slept in here at one time. My bed was that one." He pointed across the room. "The one by the window there. Those were heroic days. Hectic. But heroic. Slaying deranged beasts that attacked villagers, protecting the weak. We were busy men in those days."

"Sir Donald," I asked tentatively. "What's going to happen to my training now that the Chosen Hero is here."

"Nothing," he answered.

"Nothing?" I questioned.

"Aye, nothing." He scratched his beard. "Nothing changes. Business as usual."

I didn't share his confidence. For one thing, how could I possibly train with a million cameras all over the place? Or with stupid Al dancing around and posing for pictures?

"Get some rest," Sir Donald said. "Be prepared for more training on the morrow. You'll need sleep, trust me. It won't be an easy day of practice." With that, he turned and left us alone in the room. I shuffled over to a bed and unsheathed both swords, then placed them on the floor before crawling under the covers. Every muscle in my body still ached.

"Maybe he'll be gone tomorrow," my cousin said as he pulled up his covers.

"I doubt it," Luria mumbled. She stood looking outside the window, at the pinpricks of stars far in the distance. I could just make out the silhouette of a mountain range blocking the stars on the horizon. Moonlight drifted inside, highlighting her profile.

She stood with resolute confidence, her shoulders back and head held high. I admired that about her. I admired her strength. She'd leaned her staff against the wall, and its crystals gave her a soft purplish glow.

Luria looked so striking standing there with her raven hair flowing down her back, but her eyes were troubled. I wondered if I'd ever see her without a cloud of fear darkening her eyes. I almost told her to lay down and get some rest. She'd need it before tomorrow, too, but I couldn't bring myself to do it.

She was more beautiful than any girl I'd ever met, even with the curved ram's horns spiraling from her head. Not long ago, the sight of her frightened me. But not now. Now, the sight of her intensity and confidence gave me the motivation to keep moving forward.

She'd kissed me once, just on the cheek, but it was a moment that shone as a bright spot in my memory. I couldn't let her down. I couldn't let the Wraith King continue to torture her people and transform them.

I couldn't let the Wraith King win.

I also couldn't let Kyrie stay as a crow for the rest of her life. I imagined all those other people in Kroy Wen City being turned to wraiths. Who was really going to stop them? Alexander Bravestone? The thought wasn't only laughable, but also frightening. It meant the government had given up. They were doing nothing to stop this crisis but televise meaningless showy programs. They were trying to lull people into a sense of comfort while the Wraith King continued gaining power.

I drifted off to sleep with thoughts of wraiths on my mind, and I regretted it.

Red eyes peered into mine, though I saw only mist in the place of his body, and I knew I looked into the eyes of the Wraith King.

"*Shia'va,*" he whispered with a bone-chilling hiss. He'd called me that before. It was right after I'd taken the sword and he'd appeared as a mythriwraith.

"*Shia'va,*" he repeated.

Fandalore had told me it was a Druidic word that meant Chosen One.

"Your quest does not take you any closer to me," the Wraith King said in a substantial voice. Not whispers. "Why have you stopped trying to find me?"

He'd never spoken to me like this before. He'd always just hung out in the shadows, lurking, making me afraid, whispering a creepy word here and there. What had changed to make him start talking to me? The answer came almost as soon as I'd thought of it. Because I had the sword, and now he took me seriously.

Mr. Moneymaker was wrong. There was more to the sword than just its historic value.

"You want me to find you?" I asked.

"Of course." His form grew more substantial. The white bones of a skull glinted from his head like a crown, and my only consuming thought was that this was rumored to be the skull of his own father. It was such a repulsive image that a wave of nausea turned my stomach.

His clothing was different from what I'd seen him wearing in the past. Instead of tatty robes, red leather armor molded around his muscular frame. A breastplate studded with gleaming iron spikes reflected in the moonlight streaming from the window. It was the kind of clothing a person would wear for war. He stood at the foot of my bed, watching, red eyes like twin blazing orbs in the darkness.

Fear skittered down my spine, freezing me in place. The Wraith King moved to the side of my bed in a blink and hovered above me. He held one clawed hand over my chest, then he inhaled deeply. "I enjoy feeling your fear..." he drew out the last word.

My fear? Yes. The only emotion he could still comprehend. If he enjoyed my fear, then I wouldn't give him any more reason to be here. I forced myself to look away from him, to imagine anything but him. My magi-box back home. My friends who'd been waiting ages to play. My parents and sister, when we'd go to glimmer sphere ballgames. My cousin's laugh. Luria's kiss. Every happy moment I'd had in my life, I thought of it then.

When I turned back to the side where he'd been standing, he was gone.

Chapter 10
THE THIEF

I thought my muscles were sore yesterday. Today was a jillion times worse. As soon as I woke up, moving became the most painful thing I'd ever done. I somehow managed to pull myself out of bed and stumble to the bathroom. Getting washed up and changing clothes was just about as hard as pushing thirty giant boulders up an enchanted hill.

"Oooouuuucch," Maharani groaned as he trudged down the hallway behind me.

"You too, huh?" I asked.

"My toes are sore. Who has sore toes?"

We stopped outside our bedroom door, and I shook my head and closed my eyes. When I did, I saw a pair of glowing red irises looming in the dark space behind my eyelids.

"You okay, cuz?" Maharani asked. "You looked scared for a second there."

"I'm..." I ran a hand through my crazy messed-up hair. I debated on shrugging off his question. Couldn't I just tell him I was fine? But I'd always found it easy to confess anything to my cousin, so I let it slip what happened last night.

"You saw him?" he questioned. "Again?"

"Yeah, but it was worse this time. He was talking to me, like having a conversation. It wasn't just whispers and stuff."

"And he said you were the Chosen One, right?"

"He called me Shia'va again, which I guess means Chosen One."

"But why did he appear to you?"

"Honestly?" I questioned. "I think he just wants to scare me. I think that's what he wants from a lot of people. I don't know for sure, but I think somehow fear makes him stronger."

Luria opened the door and stepped out of the room. Her eyes were swollen and tired, as if she'd gotten about as much restful sleep as I had.

"What are you two talking about?" she asked.

"Gordy saw the Wraith King," my cousin said. "Again."

"Just a mythriwraith," I added, attempting to act casually, not wanting Luria to think I was scared or anything.

She nodded. "Yes, it's really hard to stop a mythriwraith from appearing."

"Umm... Luria..." I hedged. "You don't think those legends are true, do you? That I'll really be killed by the Wraith King?"

"They're silly legends," she answered, also attempting a casual tone, although I heard the hesitation in her voice, and saw the flicker of fear in her eyes.

"Silly legends," I repeated. Maybe if I said it enough times, it would be true. "Are we ready to train?" I asked, hoping to get my mind off less pleasant topics.

"Ready as we'll ever be," my cousin said without much enthusiasm. "Let me grab my shield."

"And I'll get my staff," Luria said.

"And I'll need my swords," I echoed the others as we entered the bedchamber. I went to my bed, but I found an empty floor where I'd put my swords. "What?" I mumbled. Maybe I'd kicked them under the bed. I knelt and glanced under the bed, but only found a few dust bunnies. After standing, I knit my brow in confusion.

"Umm... Maharani, have you seen my swords?"

He was hefting his shield onto his back. "No, bro."

"Luria?" I asked pleadingly as she held her staff. She shook her head.

"We'll help you look," my cousin offered.

"Thanks," I mumbled as we searched the room. It was a big room after all, and all the beds looked the same. I'd been so tired, maybe I'd dropped them by a different bed and forgotten. Fifteen minutes later, after a thorough search, we stood empty handed.

"Zappers. This is bad," I breathed, trying to fight off my growing panic. "It's..." I didn't even have the word. I'd lost the Hero's sword? How? I'd put it right there on the floor beside Schubert. I'd traded Grandpa's watch for it, and worse, it was the only chance I had at stopping the Wraith King.

"Let's just slow down and think logically," Luria said. "Are you sure you left the swords by the bed?"

"Positive." I ran a hand through my messy hair and spun around. "I mean... I think?" I had placed them there. I was so certain I would've bet my life on it. But if that were the case, then where were they?

"Maybe they're downstairs," my cousin suggested. "We were tired last night. You probably left them in the training hall and just forgot."

"Let's go check," Luria said and strode toward the door. Maharani and I followed her down the hallway and took the stairs to the bottom floor. The knights and Fandalore sat at a six-sided table eating a breakfast of toast, oranges, and porridge.

"Breakfast?" Sir Donald held up a steaming bowl.

"Not yet, thanks," I said, brushing past him. "Looking for something," I muttered, not wanting to admit what I'd lost. The Hero's sword. Of all the objects not to lose in one lifetime, this had to be it. Losing Schubert... well, nobody's heart would be broken about that.

"Looking for something?" Sir John asked.

"Uh..."

"His swords," Maharani called over his shoulder as he dashed past them.

We rushed from one table to the next, looking under them, looking on chairs, looking in corners and under tablecloths, but found nothing but dust. I gathered with my friends near the fireplace. Flames crackled and sparked. My heart raced, and I could barely feel the fire's heat on my too-cold, clammy hands.

The two knights and Fandalore strode toward us with troubled expressions.

"Maybe they're in the courtyard," Luria suggested. "We were out there yesterday."

"Yeah, maybe so," I said, rushing past the knights and the wizard, ignoring their uneasy looks. We dashed out the doors and into the bright morning sunlight. Thimblethorn raised his head as he laid on his straw pallet.

"Something the matter?" he asked, steam rising from his nostrils.

"My swords," I answered hastily. "Have you seen them?"

He tilted his big head. "No. Afraid I haven't."

"They aren't stuck in your pile of straw or anything?" my cousin asked.

"Certainly not." He frowned. "I believe I would have noticed if I'd been sleeping on sharpened blades."

"Wait a minute." Luria stopped in the middle of the courtyard. "Where's Alexander?"

It struck me just as she said it. There hadn't been any cameras in the Hall of Eight Tables, no people buzzing around and barking orders, and the courtyard sat empty except for Thimblethorn. All the pega-coaches and drago-drones were gone. Not even their dragon remained.

"They left already?" Maharani asked.

"Just before dawn," Sir John said as he approached us.

"But..." I started. "Why'd they leave so soon? They just got here."

"Came here for what they needed," Sir Donald answered. "Some flashy pictures, a quick interview for the news, then they went on their way."

"Any idea where they went?" I asked, unable to keep the accusatory tone out of my voice. I couldn't help but think it suspicious that Mr. Moneymaker and Alexander had gone missing around the same time as my swords.

"What's that over there?" Luria pointed. I followed her line of sight to the wall near the gates where a spot of silver gleamed. My heart leapt as I made my way toward it.

"A sword," my cousin shouted as he walked with me. When we stood over it, I frowned.

"Just one sword?" I questioned.

"Yeah," my cousin said. "But which one?"

"One way to find out." I picked up the weapon and unsheathed it.

"Why good morning to you, too," Schubert called, and I wasn't sure my heart had ever sunk any lower at the sound of his voice. "Fancy meeting you out here on the cold, rock-hard ground. Why yes, you might ask. I've been here for hours, and I've got a horrible crick in my pommel, not to mention an ache in my blade that I can't seem to—"

"Schubert," I interrupted. "Slow down. We need to know how you got here."

"Tossed out a window," he said with exasperation. "I had been unsheathed in a moving vehicle, and as we flew upward into the sky,

I was ruthlessly tossed. Tossed! A sword like me, with a history like mine, treated with such disregard. It's unthinkable."

"Schubert," Luria said, who now stood beside us along with the wizard and knights. "Who tossed you?"

"A ruthless child," he answered. "He spoke with a spoiled air about him. A buffoon in a fancy red cloak."

"Bravestone," I said darkly. "Let me guess. He had the Hero's sword with him?"

"Yes. Would you believe it?"

"Actually," I answered with a sinking feeling spreading through my chest, making my limbs grow cold. "I can."

Chapter 11
THE RIDDLE

"That traitor," Maharani yelled, his voice echoing through the courtyard. "He's no Chosen One. What *hero* would go around stealing swords?"

"He's no hero," Luria spat. "Never has been. That's why you should never hire an actor to save the world. Honestly."

"How are we supposed to find him?" I asked. "We have no choice but to go after him now. Without the sword, there's no way to defeat the Wraith King."

"Is that his plan?" my cousin asked. "Do you think he's really going to try it?"

"Who knows?" I said, shoulders heavy. "I don't even understand why he stole the sword in the first place. Mr. Moneymaker said he thought it was worthless."

"Obviously that was an act," Luria offered. "He must have been desperate to have it from the moment he saw it, just didn't want us to know. I'll bet that's the whole reason they came here in the first place."

The two knights and Fandalore stood around us.

"You found a sword?" Sir Donald asked.

"Yeah." Muscles stiff, I weakly lifted Schubert. "Not the right one, though."

Schubert scoffed. "I'll have you know, I may not be the true sword, but I'm not a weapon to be trifled with."

"Schubert," I said. "We know. You've told us." I decided now might be a good time to be polite to him. After tracking down Alexander Bravestone and kicking his teeth out for taking my sword, I was sure to make a nice long list of enemies—Mr. Moneymaker and President Falcoon to name a few. I didn't feel like making any more enemies, especially not with my last remaining weapon. "Also, thank you for telling us about who captured you. It was very helpful information."

Except for the song of morning birds, the air remained quiet.

"You're... you're thanking me?" he asked in an uncharacteristically quiet voice.

"Yes," I answered curtly. "Without you, we still wouldn't have known what happened to the Hero's sword. So, thank you."

The others gave encouraging nods, and Luria even flashed a small smile, which made butterflies flutter inside me. Warmth seeped through my veins, melting the chill I'd felt after learning my sword had been stolen.

"We still have the problem of finding Bravestone," my cousin said.

I nodded to the wizard and knights behind us. They spoke quietly to one another, too quiet for me to hear what they were saying.

"Any ideas?" I asked them. "Fandalore? Surely you can figure out where they've gone."

"You want me to outright tell you?" He shook a bony finger in my face. "No, no, no. That's not how it's done. First, I must tell you a riddle in obscure language and make you decipher its meaning. Now." He combed his fingers through his beard. "Let me come up with something clever."

"We don't have time," Luria demanded. "Can't you just tell us where he wen—"

"Ah, ah, ah," he chided. "That's not the way these things work, young gel." He cleared his throat. "Now. How about this... 'Overhead, by wing and sight, through the day, and mirrored night. Find the true sword, you shall see, where it went, and where it be.'"

I frowned. "Where it be?"

He gave a small cough. "Well, I had to force the rhyme there at the end. Yes, I know it should say, 'where it will be' but as I mentioned, I've got time constraints and not nearly long enough to come up with something more refined. That being said, I've told you everything you need to know to find the sword. Now, go." He shooed us. "Back into the castle, young pups. Things to do. A world to save. Decipher the poem's meaning, and then you shall be well on your way to reclaiming the weapon and saving our world."

We looked at him with slack-jawed exasperation.

"Go," he repeated, and we turned and trudged back inside. "Inside the Hall. Be sure to eat the hearty breakfast that I've helped to prepare. See? Wizards are helpful from time to time. Vitamins and minerals. It will help your young brains think more clearly this early in the morning."

My head swam, and I could hardly believe I was having to contemplate how to get the sword after I'd already been through so much to get it the first time. The injustice of it all felt like it would rise up and choke me.

I sat with my friends at the six-sided table as we shared a breakfast of cold porridge, dry toast, and tart oranges. I tried pondering Fandalore's riddle, but I had trouble focusing on anything but how blindingly infuriated I felt at stupid Alexander Bravestone.

"It could mean we should search at night," my cousin suggested. "Didn't his riddle say something about night?"

"Yeah," I answered through a bite of toast. "Something about a mirrored night. No clue what that means."

"We should go outside at night and use a mirror?" Maharani suggested. "A magic one, maybe?"

"Where are we going to find a magic mirror?" Luria asked.

"Maybe in the castle," I answered. "In a place like this, surely there's a magic mirror somewhere, right?"

"Maybe," Luria answered without enthusiasm. "But before we go off on an aimless quest, maybe we should think of the whole riddle." She tapped her fingers on the table. "Didn't it also mention wings?"

"Yes," I answered. "Like Thimblethorn's wings, maybe. Or Val's."

"That's right," my cousin chimed in. "Maybe we could use Val to track down Bravestone and report back on where she is."

"Perhaps," I said with a frown. "But they're using pega-coaches. They could've flown halfway across Alderfell by now. It could take Val a week or more to track them down, and then it would take even more time for her to fly back to us."

"Then there's something more to the riddle," Luria said. "Something we're missing. Think of it again."

"I can't remember the whole thing," my cousin said. "How'd it go again?"

Luria spoke up. "'Wing and sight, day and mirrored night. Where it went. Where it be... Something like that.'"

"It's pretty vague," I said. *Wing, sight, day, mirrored night*, I repeated in my head. "So, we need a mirror and something with wings. Day and night." I scratched my head. "Why couldn't Fandalore have just told us? Wizards are always vague in books, but he's going too far. This is ridiculous."

"Maybe we should start training." Luria stood and grabbed her staff. "Maybe the exercise will help us sort out the riddle."

"Good point." My cousin also stood and held his shield, but as I stood holding only Schubert, it was hard to stay positive.

All throughout training, my thoughts kept going back to my missing sword. I stumbled and lost ground more times than I could count. Poor Sir Donald had had enough by the time afternoon arrived, and he told me to go back up to my room and get my thoughts straightened out before training any more.

I laid on the big four-poster bed and studied the sprawling burgundy canopy. I felt so useless just laying here. I needed to be out there looking for my sword. We couldn't train anymore. That was obvious. Training was meaningless if we had no weapon capable of defeating the Wraith King.

Closing my eyes, I thought of Grandpa. It was at a moment like this when I would have pulled out his pocket watch and clicked the lid open. I would have asked his advice. Would've listened to the sound of his voice reassuring me that I was on the right path and doing the right thing. To not give up. But I'd traded it for the sword. What had Alexander Bravestone traded for the sword? I hoped the sword sliced his arm off. Served him right.

A knock came at the door, and Luria entered.

I almost told her to go away.

"What are you doing here?" I asked, my voice gruffer than I'd intended.

"Came to check on you." If my rude tone had offended her, she didn't let it show. She sat on the edge of the bed, propped her staff on her lap, and gave me a long look. "Need to talk to someone?"

"No," I snapped. "I'm fine."

She pushed strands of hair over her shoulder. Afternoon sunlight streaming through the window made it look so glossy, and I tried my best to ignore the sight of it. "Are you?"

"Yep," I answered with mock cheerfulness. "Peachy. Just peachy."
She laughed.

"Why are you laughing?" I demanded.

"Because you're usually so upbeat and positive. I didn't think you could ever be in a bad mood. So, Gordy Simpleton is human after all."

"Did you come here to tease me?" I questioned.

She patted my foot under the blanket. "No. I came here to tell you that I understand how you feel. It wasn't just my brother and father who were stolen from me. My home and my life were stolen from me as well. I can never go back to the way it used to be. I barely escaped." Her voice had turned soft and wistful, and the sunlight streaming inside made her eyes look wild and golden, her skin as smooth as silk. I wanted to reach up and run my finger over her face just to see if her skin was as warm and smooth as it looked, but I immediately banished the idea.

Stupid, Gordy. How can you even be thinking of Luria that way at a time like this?

"I was pondering Fandalore's riddle," she said, her voice still soft.

"What about it?"

"The mirror. It's the only concrete thing he mentioned besides the sword. I was training downstairs and saw Maharani polishing his shield, and it hit me."

"You think my cousin's shield might be the mirror?"

"Yes, it's possible," she answered.

"If that's the case, then how does it relate to flight?" I tapped my fingers on the bed cover. Trying to think with the scent of honeysuckles perfuming the air wasn't an easy thing to do. "If flight refers to Val..." I sat up. "A scrying screen."

Luria lifted an eyebrow.

"Maybe Maharani's shield can be magically linked to what Val sees. We could send her out to scout the area, and we could see what she sees through the shield."

Luria didn't outright reject my theory, which gave me hope. "You might be on to something."

"Yeah, I hope so. We just need to find a way to connect the shield with my sister's sight. I have no idea how that's done."

"I think I can help with that." Luria twisted the staff in her lap. "See?" she said with a wink. "Told you that you needed to talk to someone." She leaned in and brushed a kiss on my cheek.

I froze on the spot.

Maybe it meant nothing at all. Maybe it was customary for Haemons to kiss each other at times such as this, just a friendly gesture meant to cheer me up. No matter what her intentions, I wasn't prepared for the absolute onslaught of butterflies dancing in every conceivable direction through my stomach.

She turned to stand. I wasn't exactly sure what I was doing when I grabbed her hand.

"Umm... Luria?"

"Yes?"

"Thanks. I needed to talk to someone. I'm glad you came."

She only nodded.

I wanted to say more. So much more. How did people do this? Telling a girl how you felt was just about the most ridiculously impossible thing I'd ever contemplated doing in my life.

She left before I got the chance to say anything more.

Chapter 12
THE CHASE IS ON

We stood outside the castle in the crisp morning air. Thimblethorn gave a great yawn as he stood nearby. "Too early," he mumbled as we gazed toward the mountains, their peaks covered in a layer of stark white snow. The sun hadn't risen high enough yet to illuminate the mountains, making them look lifeless and gray, as if without the light, they had no color, no life. Val sat perched on my arm and ruffled her feathers.

Maharani stood with his shield propped against his legs. "Are we ready?"

"Yes." Luria twisted her staff, making its purple crystals flash in the morning sunlight.

I glanced back at the castle, which looked like a gray speck on the horizon behind us. The knights had given their farewells and well-wishes, then escorted us out as far as the gates, but not a step outside, making me wonder if they could leave. Maybe they only stayed alive as long as they stayed in the confines of the castle.

Fandalore, as usual, was nowhere to be found.

"Luria," I asked. "Do you think you can use your staff to make the shield become a scrying screen for Val?"

"No." She shook her head. "My staff is useless for something like that. But..." She tapped her fingers on her lips. "The knights did teach me a little magic that doesn't involve my staff. I wonder..." She knelt by the mirror, then ran her hand along the shield's edges, and over the symbol of the tree etched on front. She murmured a string of musical-sounding words, until the shield began to glow blue.

I held my breath.

"Bring Val," she called to me. I walked with the crow on my arm until I reached Luria, then I knelt.

"Let her look at the shield," Luria instructed as she moved back.

I brought the bird closer until she was inches from the gleaming metal surface. Val looked into the mirror with her beady eyes, and held perfectly still, as if transfixed.

"Caw..." she sang softly, more a hum than her usual screech.

The wind blew, stirring the grass around us with a sound so musical, I felt it deep within me.

"Cawww..." The bird's voice mingled with the wind to create a symphony.

"I hear you," Luria murmured reassuringly, then stroked the crow's silky feathers. "You have a voice."

Sadness struck me. Yes, being a crow was much better than being a wraith, but how long would my sister remember her life as a human? Remember how she loved to swing and the taste of strawberries? Remember how much she adored our father and loved baking rainbow chip cookies with Mom in the kitchen? So many memories. How many had she been able to keep?

"Let her fly," Luria instructed me, and I nodded, then stood and lifted my arm. Val flapped her wings once and leapt off my arm, then soared upward, past the scattered treetops, and into the blue sky.

"Look," my cousin said. And we turned to face the shield. Instead of showing a reflection of the surrounding countryside, was saw tree-tops and blue sky, and beyond that, the mountains.

"It's working," I breathed, not daring to take my eyes off the shield.

"Does she know where to go?" my cousin asked.

"No idea." I watched as she soared over a cliff and a valley dropped beneath her. "Is there some way we could tell her what we're looking for?"

"Yes." Luria nodded to the shield. "Maharani, put your hands on both sides of the shield, then focus on where you want her to go. The more specific you can be about it, the better."

"O—kay..." he drew out the word, speaking hesitantly. "But I've never really used magic before. Not like this."

"But it's your shield," Luria instructed. "The magic will work more reliably if you control it."

My cousin took a deep breath. "All right. I'll try it." He knelt by the shield, then placed both hands on its edges. "Hey, Val. It's uh... it's me." He glanced with a pleading look up at Luria. "How do I know if it's working?"

"Concentrate," she said. "Close your eyes and focus."

He nodded, then focused on the shied again. "I... we..." He tapped his fingers on the smooth metal surface.

"You got this, cuz," I said softly.

"All right." He straightened his back. "I got this," he repeated and closed his eyes. "Val," he said with quiet confidence. "It's me. Your cousin Maharani. Remember me? We used to run around your house together playing dragon eggs. You'd get so mad because I'd pick pink every time and that was always your color. Anyway, we need your help. We need you to find Alexander Bravestone. He stole the Hero's sword.

We have to get it back if we want to save you and every other person in Alderfell. Do you understand?"

The scene on the shield remained the same. Maharani drew back and looked up at us. "Do you think she heard me?"

"I don't know," I answered. "I guess we'll find out."

"She keeps heading straight for the mountains," Luria said, not taking her eyes off the shield. The blue sky darkened as clouds gathered on the horizon, and the mountains grew larger as she neared them.

"Are those the Dragon Wraith Mountains?" I asked.

"Yes," Luria answered, then pointed to a switchback trail. "And that's the path to the Haemon caves. I'm almost sure of it."

A chill crept down my spine. "What if that's where Bravestone is going? What if he's intending to confront the Wraith King?"

"If so, then we have no choice but to follow," my cousin said. "Even though..." He trailed off and scratched his chin. "Aren't those mountains full of dangerous creatures and traps and stuff? Not to mention, they're a maze."

"But we've got nothing to worry about, right?" I asked. "Luria knows the way through. And I'm sure she's familiar with all the traps and creatures."

She shook her head. "You forgot I recently escaped from the mountains because the Wraith King was transforming my people. If that's where Bravestone is going, he won't be safe. We won't be safe either."

"But people are being transformed everywhere," I said. "The caverns won't be any different from the streets of Kroy Wen. You heard what my mom and Uncle Harlowe said. Nowhere is safe anymore."

"But why is Alexander Bravestone going?" my cousin asked. "Surely he doesn't intend to really kill the Wraith King?"

"I don't know," I answered. "Most likely he doesn't understand the danger, and his handler wants a nice backdrop that doesn't look photoshopped. Whatever the case, we've got to find him and get that sword back before he does anything else stupid."

"Val landed." My cousin held up the shield, and evergreen tree branches swayed in her vision. "And she's found breakfast." He grimaced as she held a mouse in her talons, and I glanced away.

"Gross," I said. "She's really going to eat a mouse? Because I'll give her such a hard time when she's back in her human form."

We shouldered our weapons and packs. Thankfully, we were traveling more prepared this time, and had stocked up on food and provisions before leaving the castle and heading off on our journey.

Thimblethorn lumbered along behind us. We found an old trail weaving downhill through the grass. Boulders blocked our path in places, although the sky remained clear, and the air held the fresh scent of greenery.

"Maybe Bravestone will get transformed by a wraith before he even reaches the mountains," I mused as midday approached.

"Doubtful," my cousin said. "He's got a whole security team with him. I doubt they'll let a wraith get within ten feet of him."

Luria straightened her cloak as she walked beside me. "Let's hope he doesn't try to confront the Wraith King. I can't even imagine what would happen. Bravestone would get killed for sure, and then the Wraith King would have the true Hero's sword. Imagine what the Wraith King could do with a weapon like that? With that amount of magic? It would be a disaster."

"I wish we could get there faster," I said, urgency in my voice. "It could take us days just to reach the mountains, and who knows how long to get through them."

No one offered any advice about our problem. The rails didn't run out here in such a remote place. We were stuck traveling on foot unless Thimblethorn finally found it within him to fly us there, which

I doubted would happen. On the upside, I'd been training so much that my muscles had grown stronger, and I found I was able to walk the whole day without getting overly tired. Even Thimblethorn was complaining less.

As evening approached, the landscape grew hillier, and craggy cliffs dotted the countryside. We built a fire under an overhang in a crag to block the wind, and Maharani even managed to make a broth in an actual hanging kettle he'd packed.

Holding the tin cup, I sipped the broth. The bland liquid definitely could've used more salt, although I still smiled. This was the kind of adventuring I'd read about in my books—at least, pretty close. Maybe I really could have a quest like all those past heroes after all.

"I think we're getting good at this survival thing," I offered. "I mean, better than that first night sleeping outdoors, anyway."

Maharani gave a small smile, just a hitching of one side of his mouth, but I could tell he was pleased with himself. "Yeah. It's weird to say it, but maybe it helped that we had such a miserable start, because it made me more prepared for this leg of the journey. I packed a kettle and herbs for making broth. Brought lots of nuts and seeds and even some dried fruit. Even remembered to pack an oiled cloth in case it rains again."

"Zappers." I let the mug warm my hands before taking another sip of my broth. "You're really getting good at this tracking thing."

He shrugged. "Maybe," he answered humbly, although I saw the sparkle of pride in his eyes at my compliment. After we'd eaten, my cousin pulled out a scroll from his pack and held it near the fire.

"What's that?" I asked.

"A map of Alderfell," he answered. "Sir Donald gave it to me. He said if I want to be a good tracker, I'd need better maps." I scooted close to him and looked at the faded brown parchment. The older style calligraphy denoted lakes and streams, roads and smaller paths, and the dots with words indicated towns and cities. At the western edge of the map was the ocean, and the words ALDERFELL SEA.

"I think we're here." He pointed to a path branching away from the knights' castle. "If we want to make it to the Dragon Wraith Mountains, we'll keep following this trail until we reach a river, then, we should be able to find an entrance into the caverns from there." He rolled up his map. "After that, I can't help. We don't have any maps of the tunnels inside the Dragon Wraith Mountains. That's where Luria comes in."

She nodded as she fidgeted with her staff that she held across her lap, her gaze distant. Was she worrying about guiding us through the mountain? Or was something else bothering her?

After rolling out our pallets and getting situated near the fire, I lay staring up at the sky. I looked at all those stars overhead, and I was reminded of sitting with Mom, Dad, and Luria on the back porch, looking at these same stars.

A pang of homesickness gripped me so tightly, I had to swallow a hard lump that had formed in my throat.

I'll be with them again, I had to tell myself, even if it would never come true, it was the only hope I had left.

Chapter 13
CRY ME A RIVER

The next morning arrived with a chill. Gray clouds blanketed the sky. The more we hiked, the colder it got, until patches of snow appeared interspersed on the frozen ground. Thimblethorn flapped his massive wings and breathed a breath of hot steam, warming us as we walked.

"That's a neat trick," I told him as we took a rocky path that dipped and rose abruptly.

"Yes," he said. "Dragons are well-suited for survival, especially those of my breed. We can stay warm through the fiercest cold. Quite handy, actually."

"I wonder if Opalesque Dragons can do that," I said.

"No." The big dragon laughed. "They're show dragons. Prized for their beauty. They may look nice on screen, and yes, they're beautiful, but extremely delicate. I pity the poor creature if it must be brought to this place."

As we stumbled down a steep hill, we spotted a stream cutting through the landscape. A crust of thin ice coated the surface in places. Nothing but rocks and small pebbles filled the world around us. The greenery had disappeared. The chill air stole the breath from my lungs, and the gray sky cast a pall over the already bland landscape.

"This is a good sign," Luria said. "This stream leads to the Ulinta River, which will lead us to the caverns."

As she strode forward, I noticed she walked with an air of confidence. Whatever had been bothering her last night seemed to be a distant memory. It struck me that she was suited for this weather. She drew closer to home as we got farther and farther away. Once we managed to stop the Wraith King, would I ever see her again? I'd come to think of her as a friend. She'd taught me more about Haemons than I'd ever known. She'd shown me that Haemons were real people with emotions just like anyone else.

The thought of never seeing her again was almost as bad as the thought of losing my family. Maybe my life was meant to be filled with loss. Maybe that's all I would have left by the end of this. Wasn't that exactly what the Wraith King was trying to stop? If everyone was turned to a wraith, then they would never experience loss; never experience feelings at all.

But even though loss was an uncomfortable, painful feeling, didn't it make more sense to experience it, so I'd know just how important my family was to me?

We crossed over a break in the stream and continued climbing up, over sharp rocks that cut my hands, then down steep inclines that we had to slide along to get to the bottom. The sound of gushing water came from ahead. After cresting a hill, we looked down into a deep gorge where a raging river cut through jagged rocks.

"We've got to get down there," Maharani yelled over the roaring water.

"How?" I asked. "That's a straight drop. We'll fall and break our necks for sure."

"Maybe find someplace not so steep?" I suggested.

"No," Luria said. "This gorge is steep for miles. We'll not find a better spot to get down."

Anxiousness quickened my heartbeats as I stared at the rushing white-capped water. The drop had to be more than two-hundred feet at least. And there was nothing but sharp rocks all the way down.

"I shall do it then," Thimblethorn said resolutely, catching me by surprise. We turned to stare at him.

"Do what?" I asked. "Fly?" I teased, half-hoping he'd take me seriously.

"Fly?" He frowned. "No. Slide."

I gaped at the big dragon. "Slide?"

"Yes. I shall slide down with you on my back. Those sharp stones may be deadly for humans, but they're no match for my thick hide."

"You'll really let us ride on you?"

"Yes, yes." He waved a claw dismissively, as if it were no big deal. "As long as I'm not expected to fly, I see no harm."

"Thimblethorn," my cousin said. "Thanks."

"Well, what are dragons for anyway if not to give their humans a ride now and then?"

"But..." I said. "It wasn't that long ago you were afraid we'd fall off," I reminded him.

"Perhaps," he answered. "But I think in this situation, we have no other way down the cliff and into the water. I should float quite nicely downstream as well, if you should wish to stay on my back, that is."

"Yes," we answered in unison.

"Very well then." He held out his wings until they touched the ground. "I will allow you to climb my wing to get situated on my back."

I let Luria climb up first, followed by my cousin, and then I slid into place between the two. Luria sat so close in front of me, that the honeysuckle scent of her hair filled my nose, and I had to hold my breath to keep from breathing too deeply.

Thimblethorn snaked his big head around to look at us with his wide yellow eyes. "Is everyone situated safely?"

"Safe enough," my cousin called.

"Very well." The dragon nodded. "Then away we go!"

He tucked in his wings and climbed over the cliff's edge. Although he started slowly, it only took a second before he launched his body straight downward.

The breath escaped my lungs, and I clamped my hands around Luria's waist. I felt like I was on a rollercoaster—a living, breathing rollercoaster, and it took all my willpower not to scream like a crazy person as we plunged toward the water.

We're all going to die. The thought hit me like a bolt of lightning, with fierce intensity, but nearly as soon as the thought crossed my mind, Thimblethorn held out both his giant wings. They caught the air like sails, and we glided down until we hit the water. Ice cold spray stung my legs and hands, making me realize I was very much alive.

"Cold," Maharani gasped behind me.

The swift current caught us. We barreled down the river, through the splashing, freezing spray, the noise so loud in my ears I could hardly hear anything else. Tall cliff walls rose on either side. The echo of the splashing water made it sound as if we were in a drum.

After making it past the rapids, the current slowed, and we drifted down the river on Thimblethorn's back.

"I..." my cousin gasped. "I thought we were dead back there."

"Me too," I called to him over my shoulder.

Luria sat unmoving, not speaking, as she held her staff across her lap. A bird's call mingled with the running water, and a black winged form descended on us. Luria held up her staff, and Val landed on the top, her talons clutching the amethyst crystals.

"Val," I said. "What are you doing?"

She hopped excitedly. "Caw!"

"I think she's trying to tell us something," Luria said.

She screeched in response, gave me a beady-eyed glance, then leapt off the crystals and flew away.

"Maharani," I said to my cousin. "Grab your shield. I think she wants to show us something."

He nodded, pulled the shield off his back, and awkwardly propped it on his leg. Luria reached behind her and waved her hand over the shield's metallic surface. The reflection of cliff walls became fuzzy, until they were replaced with an image of blue sky and snow-capped mountains.

"Look." My cousin pointed with his free hand. I focused on where he pointed until I saw a narrow switchback trail, and on it, a group of people riding magi-motor bikes, their blue wheels glowing against the white snow.

One of them wore a red cape that billowed behind him.

"That's Bravestone," I shouted.

"Yeah," my cousin said. "But why are they on magi-motor bikes when they had flying Pega-coaches and a dragon?"

"The air is too thin on the mountains to fly anything," Luria explained. "Plus, it's impossible to spot the caverns' entrances from overhead. This is good news. It means they haven't found a way inside the mountain yet."

"And they also don't know about the entrance we'll be taking," I said. "Maybe that means we can get ahead of them and ambush them somewhere."

"Yes," Luria agreed. "I know a few places where the tunnels intersect."

We continued floating down the river until Val returned. I gave her a pat on her head.

"Nice job spotting Bravestone," I told her.

She cawed and flapped her wings.

"Hey cuz," Maharani said with a chuckle. "Now that your sister's a crow, it seems like you two are getting along. Maybe she should stay a crow."

"No," I answered almost instantly, with a harsher tone than I'd intended. The idea of my sister being a bird forever was a thought that terrified me. "Yeah, I know being a crow is better than being a wraith, but I need her back." It was hard to explain my feelings, and I wasn't even sure I knew how to sort them out, but my family would never be whole without Kyrie. I'd never see the world the same without her—never see the slide at the fair, the swings at the park, the back porch where we'd looked at stars. It would never be the same without her there.

The splashing water grew louder. The narrow river widened as we drew closer to the base of a mountain.

"Let's get to shore," Luria called over the clamor to Thimblethorn.

He gave a nod, then climbed up the steep bank and onto dry ground. We slid off his back and dropped onto a pebble-covered beach. My clothes were damp and froze to my skin. I couldn't seem to stop shivering.

"Should we... bu-build a fire?" my cousin asked through chattering teeth.

"No," Luria answered. "It will be warmer inside the caves, and we wouldn't want to build a fire out here anyway." Her gaze wandered to the cliffs and mountains, then to the gray sky above. Everything in this place was colored in somber shades of gray—no greens or blues to be found. I remembered when Luria had gone to the fair with us, and she'd been awestruck by the colors. Now I could see why it had been so amazing.

"If there are wraiths anywhere near," Luria continued, "they'll be sure to spot the smoke."

"I also don't see any wood anywhere." I looked up the steep incline to the top of the gorge, but I saw only rocks in every direction.

"This way," Luria called to us. She motioned for us to follow. Our feet slipped over damp pebbles as we walked along the water's edge and toward a towering mountain that blocked half the sky. I rubbed my hands over my arms, trying to get warm, although nothing helped. I had the feeling that if the wraiths didn't kill us, the cold would.

The ground sloped, and we hiked down a hill that led toward the base of a mountain.

"There." Luria pointed excitedly. "See it? That's the entrance."

"I don't see anything." Maharani squinted his eyes.

"Exactly," Luria said. "You won't see it either unless you know what to look for. Haemons are great at creating camouflage. Come on." She waved to us. "I'll show you."

We followed her toward the mountain, until finally, we stopped at a boulder. "This is it." She tapped the boulder with her staff, and it didn't make a clanging sound as I would have expected. Instead, the staff seemed to pass straight through the boulder. "It's created from an illusion spell," Luria told us. "Watch."

She walked into the boulder and disappeared, then she walked back out and reappeared. "There are dozens of boulders just like this one guarding the entrances to the Haemon caves. You can tell it's an illusion boulder because of its shape. See that taller part on top shaped like an arrow?" She pointed up, and I only now noticed the arrow-shaped protrusion peeking from the top of the boulder. "Neat, isn't it?"

"Yeah," I answered. "But I'm glad you're here with us, Luria. We would've never found it."

She smiled, showing her dimples. My cheeks heated, and I had to glance away.

Maharani ran a hand through his poofy curls. "But... what about Thimblethorn? I doubt he can fit through the tunnels."

The big dragon waved a claw through the air. "Don't worry about me, young ones. You forget I'm an old dragon. I've scaled many a mountain in my days."

"But..." I wanted to argue that he'd get too cold, or the climb would be too treacherous, when I remembered how easily he'd slid down the ravine, and how the cold didn't bother him like it did us. Only a few weeks ago, he'd complained about how hard it was just to hike down a flat-paved road, and now he was willing to scale an entire mountain for us?

"Thimblethorn," my cousin said. "Are you sure?"

"Yes, yes," he said nonchalantly, twin streams of steam rising from his nostrils.

"I guess getting you out of the zoo was the best thing for you," I said.

He gave a slight chuckle. "I do seem to have gained some strength, yes, and I must admit, I do feel like a young dragon again." He stretched out his wings and gave them a mighty flap.

"You're sure you'll be all right?" I asked again.

"I shall be well enough," he answered.

"But where will we meet you?" I asked.

Luria pointed up with her staff. "Meet us at the top of the tallest cliff," she said. "That's most likely where Bravestone is headed, and it's where we'll confront the Wraith King, assuming that's where he's at."

"Very well." Thimblethorn gave a solemn nod. "Now, as it is time for us to part ways, I must bid you young heroes a fond farewell and good luck." He breathed a breath of warm steam over us. I could feel my clothes drying and my chills disappearing, then, he turned and hiked away from us. He made a sight: his big black body lumbering over the pebbled ground, his tail making swishing patterns, and a crow riding on his head.

Chapter 14
THE TROUBLE WITH TREBLES

Maharani and I followed Luria through the enchanted boulder. Magic prickled my skin as we walked through. I stared in awe at the half-translucent boulder surrounding me.

"This is so weird," I called. My voice sounded as if I was speaking in a drum. I held out my arms, feeling the tingling magic enveloping me. As soon as we stepped to the boulder's opposite side, the feeling faded, and we stood in a dimly lit tunnel.

"Look at this," Luria said, pointing to the wall. I couldn't see what she was talking about until she ran her fingers over the stone. A purplish glow shone from the rocks, creating the shape of a C with two dots.

"A treble clef. The symbol of Chaos," Luria answered. As she traced the carving, it hummed with a musical zinging. "We'll find more as we go. They'll lead us down the right path. That's how we'll find our way through the labyrinth. Since I've touched this one, the rest will glow when we get near them."

"Wow, Luria," my cousin said. "We would've really gotten lost without you."

"Not necessarily. If you happen to know the secrets of the Haemon caverns, it's easy enough to get through them."

"But that's the trick, isn't it?" I asked. "You have to know the secret. Hopefully, Alexander Bravestone will never figure it out."

"We'll know soon enough," Luria said. "Sadly, all he'll have to do is find any desperate Haemon wandering the icy wastes above us and offer enough money."

"Ah." My shoulders sank. "It's that easy, huh?"

"Unfortunately, yes. Most Haemons who live aboveground are looking for any way to earn a coin or two. Offering information is an easy way to get it. However..." Luria cupped her hands around her staff, and the amethyst crystals glowed, lighting our path. "That's assuming they'll find someone who hasn't been turned into a wraith."

Luria's staff clicked on the stone floor with every step we took. In the chilly darkness of the cavern, my clothes dried, although they were stiff and uncomfortable. I adjusted my cape, its bottom splattered in mud and holes worn through where it had snagged on briar bushes. I hardly felt like a Tevyn Brightblade.

I kept my hand on Schubert's pommel as we walked from one passageway to the next. At intersections in the passages, Luria's amethyst light revealed the treble symbols in the walls. We hiked until I was certain I would have gotten thoroughly lost if she hadn't been guiding us.

At one point, we stopped and sat on a rock outcropping. My cousin passed around leather pouches filled with nuts, seeds, dried fruit, and a few strips of jerky. As I ate, I couldn't stop looking over my shoulder, thinking that at any moment an army of wraiths would come flying at us.

"Something wrong?" Maharani asked.

"Just worried," I answered. "About the wraiths. Is it weird we haven't seen any yet?"

"Not really," Luria answered. "We're miles away from the nearest settlement. Plus, after the Wraith King transformed my people, he sent them out into the more populated areas to start transforming others. Honestly, I doubt there are many wraiths left."

I chewed on a mouthful of salty peanuts as I pondered her words. "Do you think the Wraith King really has the ability to transform every single person in the land? I mean, it seems unlikely he'd be able to get every last person, right?"

"Yeah," my cousin agreed. "You're right. People like our parents are safe inside their houses. For now, anyway. If he doesn't get every single person, then there's still hope left."

"You're right," Luria said. "For the Wraith King to be truly successful, he'll not only have to transform every living person in Alderfell, but every person in the world. All the lone islands, all the continents across the sea. Every living person. Think of it. If there's just one person left, and if that person discovers a spell like the one I used on your sister, then they may be able to find a way to transform wraiths back into people."

"Seems unlikely he'll get everyone, doesn't it?" I asked.

"Not just unlikely," my cousin said. "It seems impossible."

"Hmm..." I took a bite of my jerky. I was certain the Wraith King had already thought of that little snag in his plan. It made me wonder if he'd come up with a solution.

"But for right now," Luria said. "We need to focus on tracking down Bravestone and getting that sword back. The last place we saw him was in the southern mountains. Maharani, do you have the map?"

My cousin nodded and pulled the rolled parchment from his pack. As he unrolled it, Luria held her staff over the map, illuminating the sprawling mountains drawn on top. Luria trailed her finger over the mountains.

"There are trails through this gorge here that I suspect they'll be taking. Any other path is too treacherous." She knit her brow as she studied the parchment. "Which means they may find a way into the caverns in this area here." She pointed to a spot in the middle of the gorge. "If they do manage to get in through this entrance, then we could ambush them... hold on." She ran her fingers over the relief of the mountains, up one peak and down another. "Here, I think. It's hard to tell on a map like this where all the caverns are, but I think this will be the best place to ambush him." She pointed to a spot between two mountains. "Three tunnels converge here. They won't be able to escape if we manage to actually catch them there."

"Then that's where we'll go." I stood and slung my pack over my shoulder. We continued hiking through the quiet corridors, our footsteps the only sound. At one point, we found an underground stream and refilled our canteens. My mind kept replaying the dream I'd had of the Wraith King. He'd asked me to come and find him. Why? Shouldn't he have been trying to stop me from finding him?

My stomach knotted at the implications. What if the Wraith King needed me for something? Was that why he'd asked me to find him?

But no. I shook my head. What could he possibly need from me? I wasn't anything special. Just an ordinary kid. Not even destined to be the true Chosen One. He probably meant he needed the sword. Not me. Yes, that had to be it. He wanted the sword because it was the only weapon capable of stopping him. I doubted the sword could kill him, but it could at least imprison him for hundreds of years. If he took it, then he'd have no one to challenge him. Stupid Alexander Bravestone was heading straight for him to give him exactly what he wanted.

"What are you thinking about?" my cousin asked me.

"Oh." His question caught me off guard, and I wasn't sure I wanted to speak about the Wraith King here in these tunnels, when he could be close. I decided to turn the tables. "Not much. What are you thinking about?"

"My... people," he answered, although I suspected he'd wanted to say something else. "I'm nervous about meeting them—*if* we meet them. I'm only half Haemon, you know. What if they don't accept me? Treat me like a freak or half-breed or something? Throw me out?"

Luria, who walked a few paces ahead of us, gave a small laugh. "You obviously don't know Haemons as I do. A Haemon would never treat their own kind in such a way."

"How do you know?" he challenged. "How many half-Haemons have you met?"

"Well... none," she answered. "Except for you."

"You see?" he challenged. "It's possible that they'll throw me out, and probably do worse to Gordy since he's human."

Luria turned and frowned at my cousin. Her red-and-black scales were highlighted in the glow of her amethyst crystals. "You've been reading too many storybooks."

The tunnel widened until we entered a large, domed room with crudely carved columns supporting the ceiling. Rubbish heaps littered the stony ground. I spotted discarded rags, broken clay bowls and tankards, shoes, lumps of wax candles, apple cores and ears of corn stripped of their kernels.

Luria nudged a pile of rags with the toe of her boot. "There must have been a group of Haemons hiding here."

"I wonder what happened to them?" my cousin asked.

"I think it's obvious," I answered. "They must have all been turned to wraiths."

"But... what if..." my cousin started to say. "Maybe they were able to escape or something. I mean, there's a possibility a few people could've survived, right?"

I wanted to tell him he was being too optimistic, but I held my tongue. No need to bring up such dark topics at a time like this. We continued milling around the room, though I wasn't sure what we were looking for. Maybe evidence that someone had survived? Or some clue as to where they'd gone?

"Let's keep going," Luria said. "If someone did manage to escape without being transformed, they're obviously not coming back here. It looks like it's been abandoned for a while."

We followed Luria into a tunnel leading out of the chamber and into a narrow hallway barely wide enough for us to fit through. The panic of claustrophobia made my throat feel tight, so I focused on the calming lavender light of Luria's staff and took a few deep breaths. Its bobbing glow kept me rooted to reality, as if it were my only link to the world. Being inside these tunnels for too long, never seeing sunlight or breathing fresh air, would drive a person crazy.

Eventually, the tunnel widened, and the trickle of water came from ahead. We followed a sloping path that ran alongside a stream until we reached a broad lake filled with mirror-smooth black water.

"Stay quiet here," Luria whispered to us. "We don't want to wake the monsters of the lake."

Maharani and I shot each other concerned glances.

"Monsters?" my cousin asked in a quiet voice. "You didn't say anything about monsters."

"Not true," she said with a huff. "I warned you of the dangers many times."

I shrugged. "She's right."

"No," he countered. "You mentioned *danger*, yes, but you never specifically said anything about monsters."

Her eyes narrowed. "There are many monsters in the caverns, and not even I know all of them. Were I to tell you of every monster, trap, and poisonous gas, we'd be here for hours. Do you really want me to stop *here*—" her eyes flickered to the lake, "to give you a list of every possible danger?"

"I guess not." My cousin scuffed his toe over the ground. "But in the future, being a little more specific would be nice."

She straightened, her yellow eyes flashing with an edge of danger, making a twinge of fear prickle my skin. "Fine," she bit out. "How about I be more specific right now? The caverns are dangerous. There are many beasts in these tunnels that can kill you, and that's if the wraiths don't find you first. There are traps set by my people, gases that will suffocate you, and beasts that will rip you limb from limb. Is that warning enough?"

She didn't allow us enough time to answer as she spun away from us, her cloak swishing, then hiked along the lake's shore.

"I didn't mean to upset her," my cousin said to me in a hushed voice.

"I know."

"I just don't understand why she couldn't have been more specific sooner?"

I watched her walking with confidence, her form moving lithely around boulders and navigating over smaller stones. "I think because she forgot how foreign we are to these caves. You have to remember, except for us, everyone she knows is familiar with the monsters in the caverns. It's probably common knowledge for a Haemon. For the first time since we met her, she's in her element, and we're the outsiders."

"I guess you're right," my cousin admitted, then, after a pause. "It's not easy being an outsider, is it?"

"No, but maybe it's best for us to experience it, so we'll know how Luria feels."

"Yeah, I guess so."

We continued following Luria around the water's edge, and it made me realize what a huge lake it was. It was so big I couldn't see the far shore. A few ripples broke the surface, and my imagination went into overdrive as I imagined what kind of creatures would be living in a place like that.

Finally, we left the lake behind and entered another tunnel, the symbol of Chaos lighting our path with an eerie purple glow. The C-shaped symbol burned my retinas, and I saw it whenever I blinked.

I wondered what time of day it was. Surely, we'd been walking all day by now. It had to be near evening. But without the sun to give us any direction, I lost all sense of time. We could have been wandering just a few hours, or it could have been days.

We walked at an unrelenting pace, Luria moving forward from one tunnel to the next, never hesitating to turn down one path and then another.

"We should be nearing the intersection of the three main tunnels," she whispered over her shoulder, then stopped abruptly. Maharani and I almost ran into her.

"Is something the matter?" I asked.

"Shh..." she quieted me. "Listen."

I strained to hear anything, but I heard only the rhythmic pulsing of my heartbeat that sounded too loud in my ears.

"Voices," she said, then pointed with her staff to a tunnel on our left. "That way."

"Are you sure?" I whispered.

She nodded. "More than one person, I think."

"Should we go to them?" I asked.

"Depends on who it is," my cousin said. "What if they're wraiths?"

"Wraiths don't have conversations like we do," Luria said. "They'd never have any reason to speak to each other for an extended length of time."

"She's right," I said. "They only say a word here and there."

"Then it's either a group of Haemons or..." my cousin trailed off.

"Or Bravestone," I finished for him.

"Let's go check," I said. "Quietly," I added.

Luria and Maharani nodded their agreement, and we snuck into the tunnel. I walked on the balls of my feet to stay quiet, but even the smallest noise sounded too loud in my ears. Firelight flickered from up ahead, and I finally heard the voices Luria had mentioned.

"...just ahead..." someone said.

"Not prepared," another person chimed in, though I didn't recognize the voices. Perhaps they were Bravestone's guards speaking?

Something fell with an ear-splitting clatter behind us. I spun around to see a sea of collapsing rocks. The stones created a wall that blocked the path behind us. Dust choked the air, and I coughed as it entered my lungs. I rubbed at the grit that got stuck in my eyes. We staggered forward in the only direction we could go. Straight ahead.

Two figures emerged from the clouds of billowing dust. Two Haemon men as tall as Uncle Harlowe blocked our path. With grim faces, they pointed their sharpened spears straight for our hearts.

Chapter 15
AMBUSH

"Weapons," one of the men hissed. "Drop them."

I swallowed the knot of fear lodged in my throat. Luria was first to place her staff on the ground, then Maharani removed the shield from his back and laid it on the ground with a loud thud. I grudgingly grabbed Schubert's hilt, realizing his mouthiness would likely get us killed. But what other choice did I have but to unsheathe him? Those two Haemon warriors had danger written all over their black-and-red scaled faces. If I'd thought Luria seemed threatening, that was nothing compared to these two.

"Well, hulloo," Schubert called. "About time. I had nearly suffocated in that sheath. Do you know it smells of sweaty socks? Yes. And I was stuck in there. With that odor. For days. *Days,* do you hear?"

"Schubert," I said with a sharp tone. "Not now."

"Not now?" he questioned. "Not now?" he repeated louder. "How dare you? I've the right to be heard. I've been trapped in that foul-smelling stench pocket for days with nothing to do but contemplate my accomplishments—and even *I* get tired of such thoughts after so long."

"Schubert," I hissed through clenched teeth. "Just be quiet and look around. We're not alone."

I had no idea how a sword could see anything, as it had no eyes. A magical spell, maybe? But when I mentioned we weren't alone, he stopped talking.

"Good gracious," he said in a subdued tone. "Are those Haemon warriors?"

"Yes," I answered. "Yes, they are. And they've asked that we place our weapons on the ground, which was what I was just about to do." I gingerly placed the sword on the ground, then took a step back to stand by my friends.

One of the men marched forward. He wore his long hair in braids strung with beads that clinked as he walked. He grabbed Luria's staff and my cousin's shield, though he eyed the sword before also grabbing it up.

"I say," Schubert said in a pleasant, polite voice. "It's been quite some time since I've been handled by a fierce warrior such as yourself. Ah, if you would be so kind, please handle me with care, I'm quite an antique and you wouldn't want to—"

The warrior tossed the weapons in a heap on the ground, and they landed with an echoing clanging sound that reverberated through the small cavern room.

"Your sword," the man said as he approached me. "Talks too much."

"Yes," I answered, looking at my feet. "I know."

"You." The man pointed at Luria. "Are Haemon. What are you doing with these lowlanders?"

Her back stiffened. "Who my traveling companions are is my business. I could ask you the same question. Who are you?"

The man with the long hair shot a dark gaze at his companion, who wore his hair cropped short.

"I am Kalize," said the warrior with shorter hair. "Clan Chieftain. And this is my brother." His fur robes rustled as he pointed to the other Haemon man. "He is called Zarahemna. Now, we have told our names. It is time to tell us yours."

"Not until you tell us what you're doing in these caverns." She spoke with boldness. "If you're a chieftain, where is your clan?"

The man with the braided hair—Zarahemna—threw back his head and laughed. "Spoken like a true Haemon. Aye, you've a right to know our business, as long as you're no servants of the Wraith King."

"If you're smart, then you'd know we're no servants of his," Luria answered. "We're not wraiths, are we?"

"Aye, not for now, anyway," Zarahemna said.

"And we don't have any intention of becoming wraiths," my cousin added.

Zarahemna tilted his head as Maharani spoke, as if trying to decide who my cousin was.

"We're on a scouting mission, if you must know," the chieftain said. "We're trying to see if any of our clan is still hiding in these tunnels. Many of them escaped here when the transformations started. We're a remote clan and live on the shores of the northern lakes. The Wraith King attacked the southern clans before attacking us, which gave us time to prepare. Many of our people went into hiding. A few stood and fought."

His brother straightened his spear and rammed its end into the stoney ground. "We protected our people as long as we could, but we were no match for the wraiths. Our village soothsayer used a spell to disorient the wraiths, giving us a chance to hide in the caves."

"Our clan has been separated ever since," Chieftain Kalize said. "Although a few of us have reunited in a secluded area aboveground."

"Have you seen any of our people?" Zarahemna asked.

"No," I answered. "Although we did find a cave with some old things in it. Someone must've been there, but I suspect it was days ago."

Zarahemna nodded.

"That brings us back to you three," the chieftain said. "Why are you wandering these dangerous caverns by yourselves? Where are your parents? And why are a human and a half-breed..." He tilted his head. "Satyr...? Wandering with a Haemon?"

"I'm half Haemon," my cousin said.

"Haemon?" the chieftain said, then drew his brows together. "Interesting."

"We'll tell you what we're doing here," Luria said tensely. "After you return our weapons to us."

"In a show of goodwill, of course," I added in a polite voice. "Not because we mean to use them against you." I shot Luria a dark look.

"The staff and shield shall be returned," Zarahemna said. "The sword stays with us."

"Fine," I said with a shrug. I didn't say it out loud, but he could keep Schubert for as long as he wanted. Indefinitely, if possible.

"It looks much like the Hero's sword." Zarahemna said as he picked up Schubert and inspected the blade. The chieftain passed Luria's and Maharani's weapons back to them. "Yes," Zarahemna continued. "Same simple craftmanship. Same cross-guard that I've seen in every text on historic weaponry. A very convincing replica."

"The best," Schubert said smugly. "There is no closer lookalike than me."

Zarahemna's eyes darkened. "Is it always so vocal?"

"Yes," I answered. "Always. Which is why I keep him sheathed as much as possible."

"I take offense at that," Schubert announced.

"I'm not surprised," I answered back.

A smile flickered across Zarahemna's face. "The village children would be quite amused with such an enchanting relic."

The chieftain gave us a guarded glance. "You still have not told us why you're here."

"We were following someone," my cousin said. "A person who stole something very valuable from us. We were planning to get it back."

Chieftain Kalize raised an eyebrow. "This thief came here to the Dragon Wraith Mountains?"

"Yes," I answered. "We'd hoped to ambush him."

His eyes narrowed with suspicion. "Whatever would drive this thief to come here of all places? These wastes are deadly, especially to outsiders who don't know our secret paths through the mountain."

I traded glances with my friends. I wasn't sure how much I should tell the two Haemon warriors, except I knew we needed any help we could get at this point. Maybe it would be best to trust them. Since they hadn't been transformed, it wasn't likely they were working for the Wraith King.

"The thief's name is Alexander Bravestone. He's posing as a Chosen Hero and is planning to confront the Wraith King. At least, we *think* that's why he came here. Regardless, he stole a sword from me, and I plan to get it back. No matter what."

"This sword," Zarahemna said, still holding Schubert, turning him one way and then the other. "Was valuable to you?"

"Yes," I answered. "You may not believe it, but the stolen sword was the Hero's sword—the real one."

"Ah," the chieftain said as he rubbed his scaled chin. "I see. Now, this is starting to make sense. You..." he gave me a long look, from my scuffed boots to my blue cloak and up to my cropped blond hair... "are the true Hero?"

"I wish," I said with a sigh. "But no. I'm not, and I can never be."

"Even so," Luria added. "He did manage to get the Hero's sword from the dungeons beneath the Elderhurst ruins."

"So..." the chieftain drew out the word. "You are meaning to confront the Wraith King with the Hero's sword, although you aren't the true Hero?"

"Yes, more or less," I said with a sigh. "And we intend to do it soon, because not only did my sister get turned into a wraith, but so did Luria's father and brother."

The chieftain gave a sympathetic nod. "Yes, many of our clan have been transformed as well. If you wish, we will allow you to take shelter in our encampment, and we will aid you in searching for the thief."

"You will?" my cousin asked excitedly.

"Yes," the chieftain answered. "Unfortunately, we cannot do more than this, as we must soon continue the search to find the rest of our clan."

"We understand," I said.

"Very well." He waved toward a tunnel behind him. "We shall escort you to our encampment, but go quietly," he warned. "The tunnels ahead have been unstable since the attack."

"Attack?" Luria questioned. "What attack?"

"A bomb," Zarahemna answered. "We don't know who was responsible, but two days ago, a blast destroyed half the mountain. Thankfully, it didn't kill anyone, but it took out many of our main passages."

"Mayor Wren," I said bitterly. "It must have been her. She went through with the attack after all."

"But why?" my cousin asked. "Wasn't she supposed to be going along with the new plan to promote the fake Chosen Hero?"

"She must've done it quietly," I said. "Maybe hoping to take out the Wraith King quickly before anyone could oppose her."

"Which means she has zero confidence the Chosen Hero plan would work," my cousin said.

"Yeah." I bit my lip, picturing Mayor Wren and her lemon-yellow hair and pointed elven ears, her eyes shrewd, her glances sharp enough to cut through glass. She'd struck me as a person who was willing to do whatever it took to secure her agenda, even go behind the back of the president if she thought it was necessary.

"But did she succeed?" my cousin asked. "Did she stop the Wraith King?"

"No, of course not," the chieftain answered. "The bomb wasn't even close to his chamber."

"And even if it was," I said. "It wouldn't have killed him. The only thing that can stop him is the sword Alexander Bravestone stole from me."

"I don't understand." Maharani crossed his arms. "Why would the mayor use the bomb if she knew it wouldn't kill the Wraith King?"

"That's the thing," I said, running a hand through my hair. "No one realizes how powerful the Wraith King is. They don't read the ancient books. They think like modern people with modern problems. They forget that the Wraith King is undead—that he can't be killed with traditional weapons like bombs."

Zarahemna nodded. "You're unusually wise for one so young. How can this be?"

I shrugged. "I read a lot."

"The young human is right," Chieftain Kalize said. "The low-landers have become too comfortable with their modern lives. They have forgotten the old ways—ancient spells and true magic that comes from the earth, not the magic produced in a factory. They have forgotten how the natural world works."

"Even so, what does this mean for us?" Luria asked. "Will we be able to get through the tunnels back to your camp?"

"Yes," the chieftain answered. "Though the path will be a treacherous one. We must use great caution. Many caverns have collapsed or been blocked completely."

The two Haemon warriors turned and guided us down a tunnel behind them. The dark passageway was lit only by Luria's staff and the runes glowing along the walls. The trickle of water came from somewhere far in the distance.

A chill that I couldn't shake had settled deep in my bones. Something about being in this place, where the Wraith King had roamed, made it impossible not to think of red glowing eyes following me. I had to force myself to stop looking over my shoulder, imagining his freezing breath on my neck, his footsteps a hair's breadth behind mine.

In one area, we traversed a narrow bridge made of natural stone. On either side was a drop so deep, I couldn't see the bottom. In another area, a host of winged reptilian creatures attacked, though we made quick work of cutting them down and leaving their corpses behind.

In other areas, we found signs of the attack—rocks blasted to bits and blackened, the ground unstable and crumbling beneath our feet.

We must have walked halfway into the night when we finally emerged onto a snowy field lit by moonlight. Razor-sharp peaks rose around us in every direction. The cold stole the breath from my lungs and made my exhalations look like puffs of white clouds.

I walked behind the others, my feet dragging through the snow, as I hugged my cloak around me. Ahead, I spotted a collection of huts with roofs made of animal skins and roughly-hewn log walls. Thin streams of smoke drifted out of the chimneys, and the earthy scent of charred wood made me long for the warmth of a hearth.

We followed the two Haemon warriors through the huts until we arrived at a larger structure. Piles of wood had been stacked near the doorway, and the snow had turned to slush on the trail leading to the door slung with animal hides.

"Through here." Chieftain Kalize held the hides aside as he escorted us in. We stepped into a cheery room filled with the glow of warm, flickering firelight. Several Haemons gathered on rugs around the circular firepit.

"Papi!" a child shouted as we entered the room. The chieftain grabbed the little girl and picked her up, then held her tight to his chest. He smiled as he patted the tiny pair of horns peeking from her black hair.

"Maeli," he said brightly, his eyes smiling. His expression reminded me of Dad, of all the times he'd walked into the house after a hard day of working at the factory, his clothes wrinkled and eyes filled with exhaustion, yet he still managed a bright smile for me and Mom and Kyrie.

I wanted that again. How was it that I'd taken all the good things in my life for granted? Now, I'd give anything just to go back to the way things were, to see Dad's face light up as he walked into the room.

The two women stood and went to their husbands. After embracing, one of the women shot us a guarded glance.

"They're friends," the chieftain explained. "We found them in the caves."

Her eyes turned shrewd and distrustful. "One Haemon, a human, and..." Her gaze snagged on my cousin, with his curved ram's horns that looked Haemon, and his smooth, scaleless skin.

"Half-Haemon," my cousin answered.

"Half?" She tilted her head and pursed her lips.

"Yeah." Maharani didn't look at the woman as he spoke, and I noticed his cheeks had reddened. "Umm... Mom was Haemon. Dad's human."

"I see," she answered tensely. "I've never seen anyone like you before."

"Oh," was all Maharani managed.

"We're cold, Ariah," the chieftain said, breaking the tension.

She nodded. "Come." She motioned to us, silver bracelets jangling on her arms. "Warm yourselves by the fire. We have some leftover stew. It's not much, but it's better than nothing." She turned and left through a door flap at the back of the room.

Maharani, Luria, and I gathered around the fire. The children skipped around us. Most of them focused on me and my cousin, looking at our strange, smooth skin, and my hornless head. The youngest girl, Maeli, even peeked inside my hair to see if I had horns growing.

"No horns," she shouted to the others after leaving my hair a disheveled mess.

The chieftain's wife, Ariah, returned with a few earthen clay bowls clutched in her hands. After passing them around, my friends and I sipped the steaming broth. I finished mine in several large gulps. As I stared at my empty bowl, I wished I would've taken a little more time to savor it. Maybe I would've felt less hungry if I'd at least taken the time to enjoy the flavor of the salty bone broth.

"Gordy," my cousin whispered frantically to me as he sat holding his full bowl. "I don't like it here. They're treating me like I'm a freak."

"You're not the only one." I attempted to smooth the strands of hair still sticking up.

"No, it's different for me," he insisted, his eyes darting to the adults speaking quietly in the corner, to the children dancing with excitement around us. "You're human. Of course, you'd be different. But me? They've never seen anyone like me before."

"I know, cuz," I said. "Believe me. I get it."

"No," he hissed through clenched teeth, and I wasn't sure I'd ever seen him with so much hurt in his eyes. "Don't you see? I'm supposed to be like them, at least a little bit. They were supposed to welcome me. But you saw how the chieftain's wife looked at me. I'm not just an outsider. I'm a freak of nature. I shouldn't even exist."

He clenched his bowl so tightly I was surprised it didn't shatter.

"Maharani," I said his name with a serious tone. "That's not true. Of course, you're supposed to exist."

He only shook his head, his eyes shining with unshed tears. "No. This isn't how it was supposed to happen. They were supposed to be like family... and... I don't know. It wasn't supposed to be like this."

"But we're outsiders, cuz. Even Luria's an outsider of sorts. This isn't her clan."

He only shook his head. I didn't know what to say to make him feel better. Had he always felt like an outsider? When we were younger, he'd looked different from everyone. I'd never noticed it, but had he? Had it bothered him so much that it driven him to steal the Book of Chaos to get to know more about his mom's heritage? It must have been heartbreaking to realize that even here, among Haemons, he was still an outsider.

"I don't understand why she left us," Maharani was whispering to himself. "She didn't get along with Dad. Fine. But why did she have to leave me?"

Ahh. Now this made sense. This all had to do with his mom. Had he expected to meet her here?

Luria wandered over and sat on my cousin's opposite side. "Something the matter?"

"Nothing."

She glanced at his still-full bowl.

"Nothing?" she questioned. "You've hardly eaten anything."

"Not hungry."

"We've been trekking through the caverns all day and you're not hungry?"

He only shrugged, and she looked at him with those shrewd, yellow eyes that looked far too discerning for comfort. "Maharani," she chided. "Are you upset that these people are treating you like an outsider?"

Again, he gave another shrug.

She patted his knee with her scaled hand. "This may not be what you want to hear, but there are thousands of Haemons in the world. Just like humans. There are many different clans with many ways of living and worshipping. Some who follow the Wraith King. Others, like this clan, who oppose him. If a strange human wandered into your house and expected to be treated like family, would you do it just because they happened to be the same race as you?"

"I guess not," he admitted.

"Exactly my point," she said. "Give it time."

"No," Maharani said pleadingly. "Luria, don't you see? I've been waiting my whole life for this. How can I give it *more* time? She was supposed to be here. I was supposed to meet her, and... and... " Tears sparkled in his eyes before he placed his bowl aside, then dashed outside the tent.

Luria and I traded alarmed glances before darting after him, the stares of the chieftain and his family following us. Chilly air bit my skin as we hiked into the dark, snow-filled world. Outside the shelter of the tent and away from the fire, the world transformed from a cheery, homey place to one filled with stark realities of cold and darkness.

"Maharani," I called. "Where are you?"

Something darted to our right, and Luria pointed toward a rock outcropping with the tip of her staff. "There," she mouthed, and I nodded.

A powdery layer of snow cushioned our footfalls as we neared the rocks. Sniffling came from the far side, and we hiked around the boulder to find Maharani propped against it.

"Hey, cuz," I said softly and patted his big shoulder.

"Hey," he managed through his sniffles.

"I didn't realize this would be so hard for you," I said, and he only shrugged in response.

"Maharani," Luria said in a quiet voice. "It's okay. I never knew my mom either."

He looked up at her, moonlight shining on his tear-stained face. "You didn't?"

"No," she answered. "And I know how hard it is. Always wondering why she left. Did she even love you? If she loved you, why'd she leave... yeah..." Luria's voice trailed off.

"How do you deal with it?" Maharani asked pleadingly.

"There's only one thing you can do," she answered. "Focus on the people who love you, the ones who are still there for you."

It struck me then how insanely lucky of a life I had. Sure, I hated doing chores and hated being bored even more, but that was nothing compared to not having a mom. I felt a little awkward as I stood there between Luria and Maharani, two people who came from broken families.

"Your father is a good person," Luria said. "I can tell that he loves you. He'd do anything for you."

Maharani nodded. "Yes, you're right."

"And my father—before he became a wraith—was the same. So was my brother Rhys. I know they loved me. They'd do anything to protect me."

"But now they're wraiths," Maharani said, looking up at her, as if seeing her for the first time. Was he realizing, like me, just how important it was that we help Luria get her family back?

"Yes." She bit her lip and glanced away. We stood in the open, frigid air, our breaths like puffs of white clouds, and didn't speak. What was there to say, anyway? The fragile stillness pressed in around us. Although the air was biting cold, above us spanned a million twinkling stars, and surrounding us was a snow-filled tundra that sparkled like diamonds in the moonlight.

"Let's get some rest," Luria was saying. "We'll have a long journey tomorrow trying to scout out Bravestone."

"I don't know if I can," my cousin said. "You have to admit, this journey isn't what we thought it would be. We were just supposed to help Gordy pretend to be the Chosen One. Now, we're heading straight for the Wraith King's lair with no one to help us. The government abandoned us. We can't find our wizard. Our parents are locked in their houses." He threw his hands in the air. "What are we even doing? Has anyone stopped to think about how stupidly dangerous this quest is?"

Luria and I remained silent, until finally, Luria spoke up. "That's not true," she said. "We *do* have help. We still have a dragon out there somewhere who's risking his life right at this moment to aid us, and we've found a good clan who can help us find Bravestone and the sword. I was just talking to the chieftain who said he's willing to organize a tracking party. They'll leave first thing in the morning if we're ready. There are people all around willing to help. It may not be your family, or even your own mother who's there for you, but there are good people out there, Maharani. People who love you and care about you."

"Luria's right," I said. "Maybe it's not who we want, but it's the people who want us, and those are the ones who count."

"You're right," my cousin admitted. "I know. You're right." He took a deep breath, glanced up at the millions of stars shining overhead, then turned away from them to look at us instead. "I guess I'm pretty lucky to have friends like you."

"We're more than friends," I said with a smile. "Maharani, we're family."

Chapter 16

THE WRAITH KING'S TOWER

I awoke to the sound of a child laughing, and for a half second, my mind tricked me into thinking I was home again, and that I was hearing Kyrie's playful voice. But the second I opened my eyes and saw the sunlight glowing behind the roof slung with tanned animal skins, reality came crashing down around me.

We're with the Haemons, I reminded myself. *We're inside one of their shelters, just about as far away from home as a person can get.*

"Breakfast?" a cheerful voice said beside me, and I turned to see Maeli holding a bowl of the same broth we'd had for dinner the previous evening.

"Yes," I answered. "Thank you." I took the bowl from her and sipped what little was in it, realizing it must have been hard for these people to give us their meager amounts of food. It was even more reason to leave their camp as soon as possible. They didn't need us to take all their food from them.

After getting to my feet and washing up as best as I possibly could, I joined Luria and Maharani outside the shelter. Three Haemon warriors stood with them. They wore thick fur mantles and carried spears, and with the dangerous warning I found in their eyes, I decided I was glad they were on our side.

The wind blustered. Snow particles glittered like rhinestones in a kaleidoscope. Although the air was freezing, the sun shone brightly and took away the sting from the biting chill.

Chieftain Kalize and his brother Zarahemna emerged from one of the structures. They also wore furs, carried sharp spears, and had guarded faces. The warriors murmured a few words to each other before turning to us.

"My men tell me they spotted several tracks in the snow north of here," the chieftain said. "They say these tracks could not have belonged to Haemons, because this group walked sloppily, side by side in some cases, leaving a wide trail for any baby to follow. Could this have been the humans you seek?"

"Definitely," Luria answered.

"Without a doubt," I chimed in.

"Very well," the chieftain said. "We will follow these humans and track them down, but what is your intention with them after we've found them?"

"Get my sword back," I answered.

The chieftain raised an eyebrow.

"I know," I said with a sigh, cutting my hand through the air. "That'll be easier said than done."

One of the warriors spoke up. "Do you intend to slay these human intruders?"

"No," I answered quickly.

"Then how do you propose to get this sword back?" he challenged.

"Well... I guess I hadn't thought that through exactly."

The warrior gave me a look of shrewd calculation. He must've considered me to be an idiot.

Luria thumped the end of her staff into the snow-packed ground, its purple crystals glittering in the morning sunlight. "We have our ways of dealing with him."

The Haemon warriors traded glances. "Very well," the chieftain finally said. "We shall track these intruders, but be warned, the path they have chosen is fraught with dangers. It will take us straight into the heart of the Wraith King's territory."

"That's what I was afraid of," I mumbled, and my cousin shot me an alarmed look with his eyes widened.

"He's really doing it, then? Alexander Bravestone is really trying to take down the Wraith King?"

"I suspect he doesn't have a choice at this point," I said.

The warriors moved out. We followed in single file behind them, walking in their footsteps as they tramped down the snow ahead of us. We passed through a canyon with tall peaks rising on either side of us. The imposing granite summits rose like ancient castle towers. In a few areas we found trees. Most of them were barren and leafless, their limbs white and skeletal against a depthless blue sky. A few yellow songbirds flurried from one branch to the next, and at one point, we spotted a fox skulking in the shadows of the snow-capped boulders.

We walked until the sun shone directly above us, then we stopped for a brief rest and a bite to eat. After that, the path grew steeper, and we climbed up vertical switchbacks. When we finally emerged from the canyon, I stopped, breathless, as I took in the view.

We stood on top of a mountain. Snow covered peaks surrounded us in every direction except for a huge, bowl-shaped blackened area that marred the pristine landscape. Smoke rose from some of the still-burning patches of trees. The scent of char got carried on the wind and filled the air.

I pointed to the dark spot. "Is that where the bomb was dropped?"

"Yes," Zarahemna answered.

"It destroyed a larger area than I thought."

He nodded. "The path to the Wraith King's tower will take us through a portion of the blasted area. Look there." He pointed to our left. "The sea." I followed his line of sight until I saw the glittering edge of the sea against the horizon, just beyond the mountain peaks to our west.

As I studied the edge of the horizon, a spot of black moving along the landscape caught my attention. My heart gave a fearful leap as I thought it might be a flock of crows, but as I looked more closely, I realized it was only one creature with a hide that reflected its shining scales.

"Thimblethorn," I called. "Look." I motioned to Luria and my cousin. "Look, it's him. Our dragon!"

"You're right," Maharani said excitedly. "Thimblethorn," he called, waving.

"I doubt he can hear you," Luria said.

"I know," my cousin argued. "But it doesn't hurt to try."

Zarahemna pointed to a tall cliff overlooking the sea. "Look where he's heading. He's nearly to the Wraith King's tower."

A spike of worry pricked my heart. "Why's he going there? We told him to meet us at the tallest mountain."

"He must be on Bravestone's trail," Luria said. "Probably trying to get the sword back for us."

"But he'll be killed," my cousin said, his voice panicked.

"Not if we get there first," I said.

"But how will we get to him first?" Maharani questioned. "He's too far ahead. We'll never catch up."

"Yes," I agreed. "But he's big, and he's moving slowly. If we go fast enough, we may be able to catch him in time."

Zarahemna gave a solemn nod. "We move quickly." He motioned to the other warriors, and they set off at a break-neck pace down the trail. The packed ice slipped under my boots, and I fell more times than I could count. We moved at such a fast pace, I hardly had time to notice the blasted rocks, the blackened and uprooted trees, some of them still smoking. It was like we walked through a cursed land, one covered in soot and death. The acrid scent of smoke burned my nostrils.

In some places, we found the bodies of raccoons or squirrels. In another area, we found what must have been a forest, though the trees had all been flattened. All that remained of the forest were splintered trunks sticking up like skeletal fingers from the ground.

Down the path we traveled, past the remains of what must have been houses, although now were piles of smoking logs. Only their stone chimneys gave any hint as to what had so recently been there. Cooking pots, whittled horses and birds, and bits of broken pottery lay among the smoking ruins.

Luria shook her head in disgust. "Such a waste," she muttered bitterly.

Overhead came a chorus of low, moaning wails. Several spectral figures with flowing, tattered robes in shades of charcoal black floated above us.

"Wraiths," my cousin hissed. He held his shield in front of us, although the wraiths soared as if they didn't notice us. They moved on the air current, tatty cloaks flying, until they disappeared over the next rise.

"They ignored us?" Maharani asked, lowering his shield.

"Yes," Chieftain Kalize said. "Although I doubt this is a good omen."

A spike of terror shot through me. "They're headed for Thimblethorn."

We dashed down the pathway leading through the ruined homes and buildings, kicking up a cloud of soot in our wake. My heart pounded. Despite the cold, sweat soaked through my clothes. All I could do was think of the big dragon with Val riding on his head. They'd be no match for wraiths.

We rushed until I struggled to breathe, until my muscles begged me to stop, until my feet felt as if they'd turned to anvils, but I ignored my discomfort. The path sloped down and joined with a wider road paved in cobblestones.

Ahead, at the end of the road, stood a tower that resembled a lighthouse. I could just make out the glittering scales of a black dragon starting to climb up the tower. I hardly noticed the crashing sea to our left. My heart was pounding so fast, I swore it would beat a hole through my chest. Our footsteps echoed over the broken stones.

The dragon climbed higher.

When we finally reached the tower, I could no longer see Thimblethorn.

"He's up there," I called to the others as I stood at the base of the tower. It rose at least two-hundred feet in the air. The crashing waves thundered as they dashed against the rocks beneath us, and I could taste the salty air. A narrow crumbling staircase wound around the tower until it reached the top.

I ran for the staircase when someone grabbed my arm, stopping me.

"Slow down." Luria clenched my arm. "That's the Wraith King's tower. You can't just go charging up there."

"But Thimble—"

"He can take care of himself," she interrupted. "That tower is surrounded in dark magic. If you'd stop for half-a-second, you'd sense it."

"I—" I swallowed, then looked up at the tower, its stones blackened with age. As I stood listening to the roaring wind and churning waves, the prickle of a dark, tainted magic made my skin tingle.

"Gordy, what if this is a trap?" Luria questioned.

"No." I tore my arm away from her grasp. "My sister's up there. I have to go to her."

I knew Luria's words made more sense than I cared to admit, but I couldn't let anything happen to Val. She'd already been transformed into a wraith, then to a crow. I doubted she could withstand another attack.

Footsteps echoed, and I looked down to see the others—including Luria—traipsing up the narrow staircase. The ancient stones shifted beneath my boots, and in a few places, they crumbled away completely.

What had Thimblethorn been thinking? What had driven him to climb the Wraith King's tower of all places? I wanted to call to him, but I knew the only advantage I had at this point was the element of surprise. I could imagine the Wraith King up there at this moment, waiting to take down my dragon and my sister. Was Alexander Bravestone up there, too?

If so, I hadn't seen him, which meant either he hadn't made it up to the top of the tower, or he'd made it up more quickly than we'd anticipated and was already confronting him.

Knots twisted inside my stomach as fear churned through my insides. Shouts came from above, which only made me move faster. It didn't matter that I didn't have Schubert. How useful could he be anyway? No. I didn't need Schubert. If I wanted to defeat the Wraith King, there was only one weapon I could use.

"Go now," a voice shouted above, followed by a roaring and a flash of brilliant blue light. What was happening?

I raced to the top of the tower, heart pounding and sweat dampening my empty hands. Thimblethorn lay coiled near a pedestal holding a blue jewel crusted in sparkling ice that crackled as we approached it. A chill emanated from the enchanted gemstone. Val flew to me in a flurry of black feathers, and I held out my arm. She landed with a ferocious squawk and kept her beak open as she panted.

"Val," my cousin called as he raced toward us. "And Thimblethorn."

The other warriors and Luria also entered the circular room. A few broken pillars ringed the open space, although there was no roof to speak of. I stared around the tower, shocked at finding no one there but my sister and dragon. The open sea filled the horizon to our west, and to the east were the sharp peaks of the Dragon Wraith Mountains.

"Where's the Wraith King?" I asked. "And Bravestone and everyone else? We tracked them all the way here."

Thimblethorn's head rose slowly, and it was only then I noticed the bloody wound in his neck, as if he'd been slashed with a sword.

"He's hurt," I called to the others as I hurried over to him. "Thimblethorn, what happened?"

He gave a slow nod. "I followed them," he whispered hoarsely and gave a faint smile.

"Bravestone?" I asked.

"Yes. I knew... you needed the sword. It was yours, after all. Well... I thought I'd just take it back. Found them up here. I thought it best to ask politely. No need to stir them up unnecessarily. But they laughed at me when I asked, then they gave me this nasty cut on my neck for my trouble."

"Oh, Thimblethorn." Luria ran her hand down his snout. "You poor creature. Let me see if I can fix that cut." She placed her staff aside and slung her pack off her shoulder. After rummaging inside, she pulled out a jar of salve and some bandages.

As Luria applied the salve to his wound, I sat beside his big face and patted his scaly nose. "Thimblethorn, what happened? Where's Bravestone?"

He nodded to the ice-blue gemstone glowing at the room's center. "I heard their voices as I climbed up. When I got here... they..." He winced as Luria glopped the salve on his neck.

"Sorry," she said.

"They... were standing around that ice jewel at the room's center. They were saying the Wraith King and a few of his wraiths had used it to travel someplace. The spell... it was still active, so..."

"They followed him," Luria finished for him, and he gave a feeble nod.

I sat back on my heels and scrubbed my fists over my eyes. "This isn't good. This really *really* isn't good. That was an ice spell Haemons use for traveling, wasn't it?"

Worry clouded Luria's eyes as she nodded. "I'm afraid so."

Maharani knelt beside me. "But where did they go?"

"I don't know. They could've gone anywhere in the world. And since Bravestone used the same spell to travel, he closed the passage. There's no way we can follow them."

"*And* he still has your sword," Luria added, then began wrapping a bandage around the dragon's neck.

Val flew overhead, circling us once before landing on the dragon's head, as the Haemon warriors gathered around us.

"I'll bet Val knows where they've gone," Maharani said. "That gives me an idea." He snapped his fingers. "You can show us, can't you, Val?"

She squawked.

He knelt by his shield. "Here, let's try something."

"What are you doing?" Luria asked, looking over her shoulder as she wrapped the bandage around Thimblethorn's neck.

"Testing a theory," my cousin answered. "If Val saw where Bravestone and the Wraith King went, she could have seen the place they entered through the ice spell they used. If so, she'll be able to show us her memories through the shield."

"Her memories?" I asked. "Are you sure? She's only ever been able to show us the present."

"I know this is a longshot," Maharani said. "But if the magic works to show us what she sees in the present, couldn't it also work to show us what she saw in the past?"

"I don't know, but let's try it." I held out my arm, and Val hopped from my elbow to my open palm, then she stood in front of the mirrorlike shield. The smooth surface reflected her sleek feathers and talons clutching my fingers.

"Luria," Maharani said. "Can you cast a spell that will help Val show us the past?"

She looked from the bird to the mirror. "Maharani, that's a longshot. Gordy's right, we've only ever been able to see what she sees in the present."

"But you can still try, right?" he asked.

"I wouldn't even know what spell to use," she argued.

"Just use the same one you used before," my cousin explained. "It should work the same way."

"All right," she said with hesitation, then she took a deep breath. "I'll try." She secured the bandage, then gave the dragon a final pat before crossing to us.

Luria and I knelt by the shield, and I held Val on my arm until her reflection showed in the metal's surface.

"You'll have to concentrate on what you saw," my cousin said to the bird. "We need to see where the Wraith King and Bravestone went. Do you understand? We need to follow them." He pointed to the ice-encrusted blue jewel shining at the room's center. "When they walked through the portal created in the gemstone, you should have seen a bit of the land they walked into. Did you see it?"

The bird squawked and leapt excitedly.

"I think that's a yes," I said.

"When Luria opens the shield's magic," he continued, "can you show us what you saw? Can you show us where they went?"

"Caw," she called eagerly, and it was easy to imagine my sister in the bird's body leaping up and down.

Luria nodded, then she tapped the shield with her staff. A musical tinkling emanated from the metal, like the long, echoing gong of a bell. A dense fog formed on the surface. Val held perfectly still. She stared into the fog on the shield. Its swirling mass began to take shape.

An image formed. In the fog's center shone the blue jewel, then the rest of the scene came into view.

I couldn't stop the cold shiver from running down my spine as I looked at the image of the Wraith King. The realization that he'd so recently been here was a thought that chilled me straight to my core.

The Haemon skull he wore on his head—the skull of his own father—was the first thing I noticed. Then, the glow of his red eyes, like two bloody orbs, came into focus. Although this was only Val's memory, it seemed as if he looked straight into me, as if he saw my innermost secrets. He was taunting me to follow him.

"Look there," Luria pointed. I'd been so caught up in focusing on the Wraith King, I hadn't even noticed the green jungle forming behind him. He slowly got swallowed by the jungle and the large square stones sitting among the vines. Several wraiths flew around him, their mouths open in soundless screams. Soon, the portal swallowed him, and the fog returned, but only for a moment.

Alexander Bravestone and a few of his people stood beside the blue jewel. His handler, Mr. Moneymaker, strode forward, then placed his hand firmly on the still glowing gemstone. A blue light engulfed them, and the same jungle scene appeared. This time, the square-shaped stones caught my attention, reminding me of something, although I couldn't recall what.

Then, the scene disappeared until we looked at an ordinary shield.

The Haemon warriors had gathered around us, although no one spoke.

"Where did they go?" my cousin finally asked, breaking the silence. "It looked like a jungle, but I couldn't tell where."

"Maharani," I asked. "Do you have your map?"

"Yeah, hold on." He slung his bag off his shoulder, then pulled out the scroll. After unrolling it, he placed it on the floor. My cousin, Luria, and I knelt over it.

"Where are all the jungles in Alderfell?" Luria asked.

"Here, to the south mostly." Maharani pointed to the bottom half of the map. "But those jungles are huge. How are we supposed to know exactly where?"

"The stones," I answered, and my cousin's eyebrows rose. "Didn't you see them? Big square stones. They didn't look natural." I ran a hand down my face. "I feel like I've seen them somewhere."

"You're right," Luria agreed. "I noticed the stones, too. They looked worn and old. Maybe they belonged to an ancient civilization? Were there any civilizations that shaped stones like that in any of these areas?" She pointed to the southern portion of the map.

"No clue." Maharani shrugged his big shoulders. "Thimblethorn," he addressed the dragon. "You're old, right? Do you know of any ancient people who made big square stones out of black rocks?"

"My apologies," he said weakly, his chin resting on his front legs. "I never traveled to the southlands. Bit too hot for my liking, you see. Very uncomfortable temperature for a dragon of my size."

"The black stones," I mumbled to myself. "Something seemed so odd about them." And then, as if hit by a bolt of lightning, it struck me. I snapped my fingers. "Volcanoes," I exclaimed a bit too loudly, earning me odd looks from my friends and the surrounding Haemons.

"Volcanoes?" Luria questioned.

"Yes." I pointed to the outer isles on the western edge of the map. "Look. These islands are all volcanic, but I remember reading about one..." I scanned the parchment, then jabbed the smaller island on the far left. "This one. Nambour Isle. It's rumored to have pyramids made of black glass. It could be the same kind of black stones we saw in Val's vision."

"Yes, I think you're right," Luria said.

"Even so," the chieftain said, speaking for the first time since we'd arrived at the tower's top. "How do you intend to travel there?" He nodded to the ice-blue jewel, which only reflected the light, but didn't glow with its own power. "The spell in the ice has been completed. No one can travel through it again."

We stood in silence. It seemed so unfair that everything we'd worked for had just been taken away.

"There's got to be a way." Luria spoke with fervent determination. "Couldn't we hire a Pega-coach or something?"

"There isn't a coach near us for miles," I said. "Plus, I doubt the battery would last long enough to get across the sea."

"But there's got to be a way," Luria said pleadingly, tapping her staff on the floor. "What if... what if I made the spell in the ice gemstone useless?"

I shot her a questioning look. "How would that work exactly? The spell is gone. It's already useless."

"Ugh." Luria ground her teeth. "Sometimes this staff is so useless."

"Well—" I started.

"Yes, that's its name," she finished for me. "I get it."

The chieftain paced beside us. "Even if you make it to those islands, I must warn you, there is a great curse on them."

"A curse?" Maharani asked.

The chieftain nodded solemnly. "Those are no ordinary isles. They are cursed and evil. You will never encounter such a terrifying place. I will tell you their true name, the name they have been called since the birth of time, but I will only say it once. They are... The Isles of First Birthdays."

"Umm..." I traded a glance with by cousin. "First Birthdays?"

"Sounds... uh... terrifying?" my cousin said.

"Yeah, terrifying," I echoed him. Of course, something like Skull Isles or Death Islands may have been more terrifying, but the chieftain seemed to think otherwise, so I held my tongue from challenging him.

"Do you not understand the name?" he questioned.

"Not really," I admitted.

"The first birthdays," he explained. "The first two birthdays ever. Of Chorus and his twin brother Chaos."

"Ah," I exclaimed. "Okay, that makes sense now, I guess."

"But what makes them so terrifying?" my cousin asked.

Chieftain Kalize gave us a shocked expression. "You don't know?"

Luria spoke up. "They're not Haemon," she explained. "They've never read the Book of Chaos like we have. They've learned half the truth, but not all."

The chieftain nodded. "Very well. Tell me, what do you know of the births of Chorus and Chaos?"

"Well..." I said as I did my best to remember. "They were born from the first musical notes. One could create, the other destroy. Working together, they created the world. Chaos caused the volcanoes to erupt, earthquakes to shape the land, fire and ice to rain down and create oceans.

"Then, Chorus used the destruction to plant seeds in the dirt after the fires, to shape living cells from the chemicals in the boiling oceans. On the final day of creation, Chorus used those living cells to create the races of humankind—elves, satyrs, pixies, humans, and all the other living creatures." I glanced at my cousin. "Am I getting this right?"

"Pretty much." He nodded.

"This is all you've been told?" the chieftain asked.

My cousin and I nodded, and the chieftain clicked his tongue disapprovingly. "Then you do not know the full story. But I shall tell you. If you plan to travel to the Isle, you must know it's full history." He sat on the floor, then motioned to us. "Sit," he said. "This is a tale that must not be rushed."

After we got situated, he threaded his fingers together before speaking. "The world was created as you've been taught. The first two notes of music brought the brothers into existence. The elder brother Chorus came first, followed by Chaos. Chaos destroyed so Chorus could create. There was harmony and balance between the two.

"Chorus created the first species of humankind. They lived in peace and harmony for many centuries, until those races forgot the purpose of their creators. By then, they had twisted the story of creation. They chose to believe Chaos was evil.

"They hunted and captured Chaos, took him to a faraway island, and imprisoned him in a cave. Then they left him for dead. Chorus, seeing his brother in mortal peril, went to the cave to rescue his brother. But he arrived too late. Chaos had died a cruel death of thirst and starvation. Chorus, in his pain and misery, took the bones of his brother and made his final creation. He formed a Haemon man from his left rib, a Haemon woman from the right.

"After this creation, he cursed the cave where his brother had died. Anyone who entered the cave would die. But Chorus could only create, and never destroy, so his curse filled the cavern with all his power—a twisted, cursed power, but one of immense force. Then, after expending all his life force, he, too, died in the cave where his brother had perished."

We sat in silence. "Why?" was the only question I knew to ask. "Why were we never taught this?"

Maharani only shook his head.

"Now you know," the chieftain said. "And now you understand how this island came to be cursed."

"And also, why it's so powerful," Luria remarked, frowning. "Which explains why the Wraith King went there. If he's able to harness this twisted power of creation, he'll have the ability to transform every creature on the planet into an undead with only one spell."

"Leaving no one behind to undo it," I said solemnly, a cold sweat chilling my skin at the implications.

Zarahemna walked forward and sat by his brother. "The ancient stones you saw," he said, straightening his furs. "These were most likely the remains of one of the pyramids built by the first Haemon civilizations who lived on the island."

I rubbed the heels of my hands over my eyes. It was a lot to take in. All I knew was that we really needed to get to that island.

"Right then," Thimblethorn said and attempted to stand up, his claws scratching over the floor. He winced as he straightened his neck. "I see the time has come." He stretched his wings, then extended one to the floor.

"Thimblethorn," I said, confused. "What are you doing?"

"I thought it was obvious," he answered. "I'm giving you three young adventurers a ride out to that island."

"What?" my cousin said, shocked.

"But you're hurt," Luria argued.

"A scratch." He waved a claw dismissively through the air. "The salve has already started to heal me."

"But Thimblethorn," I argued. "What if you don't have the strength to make it across an entire ocean? You could drown."

"No, no," he said with a dismissive chuckle. "You forget I've recently crossed the wilds of Alderfell and traversed the Dragon Wraith Mountains." He stretched his neck and gave a deep sigh. "I daresay I'm ready to fly again."

"Are you sure?" I questioned. "You haven't flown in years."

"A dragon is sure when he says he is, and not a moment sooner," he said with a philosophical tone. "And," he continued, "as you've been invited to ride on my back, I suggest you take the offer. It's never a good idea to refuse a ride from a dragon, especially one who's willing to take you to the Wraith King where we can once and for all be rid of him. I also wouldn't mind if you made a fool of that spoiled child who gave me this." He pointed at the bandage wrapping around his neck.

"Ah, got it," I said. His enthusiasm for flying was starting to make more sense.

"Then we should go." Luria stood and held her staff with a firm grip. "Before you change your mind."

"I agree," I said, and I also stood as Maharani got to his feet. Val flapped her wings and gave three chirping caws before flying around the tower, then landing on the dragon's head. We climbed onto Thimblethorn's back, me in front, Luria in the middle, and Maharani in the back. I gave Thimblethorn a pat on his smooth, scaled neck.

"Thank you, friend," I told him sincerely.

"Don't thank me yet," he said, then flapped his mighty wings. "Thank me after we've reached the island and defeated the cursed Wraith King."

Thimblethorn stepped to the tower's edge. Looking down, the drop seemed to span forever. I tightened my hands around the large dragon's spike in front of me as a knot of nervousness tightened in my stomach. Thimblethorn stretched his wings, but before he could leap off the tower, a voice yelled behind us.

"Wait," Zarahemna called as he rushed forward. He held Schubert as he dashed to my side. Shubert was still in a sheath, and buckles jangled from the belt where the leather case was attached. "I can't allow you to travel to the cursed isle without a weapon. Take the sword. It belongs to you. It is not meant for me or anyone else."

"Umm... thanks," I said sheepishly as I grasped the still-warm pommel, then buckled the belt and connected sheath around me. I could only imagine what Schubert would say about being returned, once again, to me. Pitiful, useless me.

"May Chaos go with you," called the chieftain as he stood behind his brother.

We nodded, then turned back to the drop, although Thimblethorn
hesitated.

I gave him a gentle pat. "You can do it."

"Yes," he breathed, steam rising from his nostrils.

With a giant leap, Thimblethorn flew off the tower. We descended
toward the ground, and I kept my hands so firmly clutched around his
spike, I thought I would break my fingers. But just as we neared the
rock-strewn ground, Thimblethorn pumped his massive wings, and
with a mighty whoosh, we rose into the air, past the tower's top, and
into the clouds.

Chapter 17
THE ISLE OF FIRST BIRTHDAYS

The cerulean blue ocean spanned in every direction. Small spots of green interspersed the water where a chain of islands dotted the seascape like jewels in a crown. The fresh air rushed past, holding the faint scent of salt. It had grown warmer as we'd flown, and I'd peeled off several layers of clothes. I was still in shock that the big dragon had agreed to fly. So far, he'd had no trouble crossing the ocean.

We flew for an entire day. When the sun sank toward the horizon, we landed on a small island filled with palm trees and white sand. Luria rebandaged Thimblethorn's wound, and we made camp for the night. The next day, we packed up and set off once again.

As midday approached, we landed on another island, and my cousin pulled out his map. "I think we're here." He pointed to a dot on the western half of the map. "These island chains are called the Satyr Isles, which means we're getting closer to the bigger islands. Nambour Island—or the Isle of First Birthdays—is here." He moved his finger to the largest island on the map's western edge. It had a vague skull shape, with two lakes at its center that could have been its eye sockets.

"We'll need to keep flying southwest," he said to Thimblethorn. "Just follow the island chains until we get to the big one."

I couldn't seem to pull my gaze away from the island inked on the page. What would we find when we got there? After a quick meal of some berries, nuts, and a few sips of water, we mounted the dragon once again. Val fluttered her black wings before flying and landing on her spot on the dragon's head, talons clutched firmly around Thimblethorn's horns. The dragon spread his wings and leapt into the air, circled upward, and back into the depthless blue sky.

We flew over a span of ocean with nothing to see but blue sky and blue sea. But as afternoon approached, a group of islands appeared on the horizon. It could have been a beautiful scene, volcanic islands filled with vibrant greenery against a pink-tinged sky, yet I couldn't push away the sense of fear that had settled deep inside me.

I felt as if the Wraith King knew we were coming. It was the same fear I'd felt when I'd had the nightmare in the tower at the Knight's castle. The terror was enough to make my skin sweaty and my stomach nauseous, and all I could think about was Luria telling me that anyone who saw a mythriwraith was bound to be killed by the Wraith King. Worse was knowing that the Wraith King expected me to come, as if I would somehow play a part in his plan to control the cave's magic.

If so, then why didn't I ask Thimblethorn to turn around and drop me off at one of the uninhabited islands? I'd swim home if I had to. At least that way I wouldn't die and break my parents' hearts in the process.

But no. How could I possibly be thinking that way? I couldn't abandon my friends to confront him alone. If I didn't do something to stop him, my sister would still be stuck in a crow's body, Luria's family would still be wraiths, and everyone else would be turned into a wraith instantly if the Wraith King harnessed the magic of the cave.

I shifted my weight on Thimblethorn's back. Riding a dragon wasn't what I expected. Although the first few hours had been terrifying, I'd gotten used to the rhythm of the pumping wings and the feeling of the constant breeze on my face.

On the horizon storm clouds billowed, and lightning blossomed in their depths.

"Look." Luria pointed. "Do you see it? I think that's Nambour Island." I followed her line of sight, looking below the blossoming thunderheads until I spotted the jagged outline of mountains that stretched across the horizon.

"Yes, I think you're right," I called back to her.

Val, still sitting on Thimblethorn's head, gave a mighty caw and flapped her wings. As I peered at the rising, jagged peaks, a whispered voice intruded on my thoughts. *I can see you*, the Wraith King's voice hissed. *You're so close. Come. Let me show you how I will end all suffering.*

Taking a deep breath, I rubbed my forehead where a headache pounded, but it only got worse the closer we got to the island. By the time we finally landed on the beach, it had gotten bad enough to make my vision go blurry. After I dismounted Thimblethorn, I was forced to drop to my knees in the sand.

"Gordy," my cousin said. "What's wrong?"

Luria knelt beside me, and Thimblethorn looked at me with concern in his huge lamplight eyes. Even Val landed in front of me and gave my knee a gentle peck.

"It's the Wraith King," I said, breathless. "He knows I'm here. He knows I'm coming."

"How do you know?" Maharani asked.

"Because..." I gasped. "I heard his voice... in my head."

Luria's eyes narrowed with concern. "You heard his voice in your head?"

I managed to nod.

"Gordy." She placed a hand on my shoulder. "That's not good. That's..."

She didn't finish her sentence, although I had an idea of what she meant to say. People who hear the Wraith King's voice in their heads don't end up doing so well—as in they get murdered by him.

Val flew up and perched on my shoulder, then pecked at my hair that had fallen into my face.

"You look super pale, cuz," Maharani said. "Here." He pulled the canteen off his belt. "Have some water."

I nodded and took the canteen from him. Although the water was cold and soothed my dry throat, it did nothing to help my pounding headache. I managed to smile as I handed the container back to him.

"Thanks," I said. "I'm feeling better." It was mostly a lie, but I didn't know how to stop the Wraith King while we were sitting here on this beach. I allowed the smell of fresh, salt-scented air and lulling sounds of swelling waves to calm my racing heart. When I felt ready, I stood up and scanned the area.

Beyond the beach spanned a forest of palm trees.

"What do you think's in there?" my cousin asked in an uneasy voice. "Were-jaguars? Giant snakes?"

"I don't know," Luria answered. "But probably."

I rubbed a sore knot in my neck. "We'll have to cross through it to find that cave. And that's assuming we can find it." I turned to Val who still perched on my shoulder. "Val, we need to find out where the cave is. The Wraith King should be somewhere nearby, as well as Bravestone and his group. Do you think you can fly over the island and find it? We'll be able to see what you see through Maharani's shield. Just be careful. Don't let anyone see you. Come back to us as soon as you can."

She gave a caw and bobbled her head in a nod, then she leapt off the dragon and pumped her wings. Her black body disappeared as she flew over the forest and toward the jagged line of volcanoes.

My cousin pulled the shield off his back and propped it in the sand. Luria gave the shield a tap with her wand and whispered a word of magic. We sat anxiously and watched as a purple mist engulfed the metal surface, then slowly cleared away to reveal the tops of the verdant green trees.

Val flew swiftly over the forest. Swaying palms gave way to fields of black rocks, then, in the distance rose a step-pyramid half covered in greenery. A stream of smoke rising into the air caught my attention. It must have caught Val's as well, because she circled lower.

In a clearing I spotted a camp of red tents and a fire burning where the smoke lazily coiled into the air.

"There," I said. "That must be Bravestone's camp."

"Yeah," my cousin agreed. Val kept flying, past the camp, and toward one of the volcanoes.

"Where's she going?" I wondered aloud.

"Maybe she spotted something else?" Luria questioned.

"Yes, maybe," I said. She circled downward. A lake of dark water reflected the setting sun. Past the lake at the base of the mountain was an opening in the rock. "That might be the cave."

An enormous dragon with flaming red scales lounged near the lake. I couldn't get a good look at it, but it must have been twice the length of Thimblethorn. "Darkfyre dragon," Thimblethorn said. "Interesting."

"What's a darkfyre?" I asked.

"Well, they were thought to be extinct," he answered. "Ancient species. Well-versed in magic. I wonder where the Wraith King found him."

My heartbeat quickened the lower my sister flew. "Don't get too close," I warned, although I knew she couldn't hear me.

A wispy form moved along the lake's shore near the darkfyre. No. Not a form. Dozens. Maybe hundreds of wraiths writhed at the edge of the lake and toward the mouth of the cave. My skin crawled at the sight of the undead creatures, their wispy gray robes, half-translucent, and skeletal faces with bits of flesh that only half resembled humanity.

And that's what the Wraith King wanted everyone to become.

The dragon looked up. Its fiery orange eyes focused on my sister flying above. It raised a claw and pointed it at her. Didn't she notice it?

"Val," I screamed. "Get away from there."

Too late, a flash of light burst from his claw's tip. Her final caw was deafening in my ears. She fell to the ground, and my heart fell with her. The last thing I saw was the undead face of a wraith peering down at her, one that was eerily similar to Luria's father.

Chapter 18
A HERO'S HEADACHE

"Val!" I wanted to jump through the shield and go to her, but the screen went dark, and we only looked at an ordinary mirrored surface. "They've got her," I said in disbelief. "They've got Val."

All I could think about was Mom and Dad, and how completely heartbroken they'd feel once I told them their daughter had been captured by wraiths.

"Gordy," my cousin said in a reassuring voice. "It's okay. We can go after her, right? I mean, we saw where she went. We'll get her back."

"Yeah." I rubbed my tender head, the headache still pounding as if I had a drum beating inside my brain. Seeing Val get captured only made it worse. "But there were so many wraiths. How are we supposed to get through them all?"

"I don't know," Luria answered in a rush. "But the wraith who captured her..." she spoke with a hint of panic. "Was that? I think it was my father."

"I thought the same thing," I told her. "But Luria, this is good news. If your father is here, it means that if we're successful in destroying the Wraith King, he'll be turned to his true self again."

"Maybe." Her lips trembled, and her knuckles turned white as she clutched the staff. "But what do we do if we fail? If we can't stop the Wraith King, which is a very real possibility, then what?"

Maharani opened his mouth to give an answer, but instead, a voice called from the forest. "About time," he shouted. I looked past my cousin to see Fandalore tottering toward us, blue robes rustling around his thin frame, his beard flapping in the sea breeze.

Luria stood and placed her hands on her hips. "Where in all of Alderfell have you been?"

"Haven't I told you never to ask a wizard such a question?" He hobbled toward us, then stopped to peer up at me and my friends. He held half a coconut and chewed noisily on a bit of its flesh. "But if you must know," he said, pointing the shell at us, making coconut water slosh over its edges. "I was setting you up for success in furtive and secretive ways that may or may not prove to be successful."

"I hope you're right," I said. "I also hope you're planning to help me get my sister back, because she was just kidnapped by wraiths."

"Plus," my cousin added. "We still haven't gotten the Hero's sword back."

"Well, of course not," he said nonchalantly. "You didn't expect to get it back too easily, did you? No. I imagine you'll only get the sword back in a grand and dramatic way. Now, as for this business of Gordy's sister, I'm sure she's in no great danger yet." He scooped out a bit of coconut and popped it in his mouth. "I've been spying on the Wraith King, and he has no other focus than on harnessing the magic from that cave. I doubt he'll waste his time killing a single crow. Not yet anyway. Not unless he has good reason to do so."

I rubbed my throbbing temples. Was it just me? Or did Fandalore's words seem to hold a double meaning? *Unless he has good reason to do so...*

What reason would the Wraith King have for killing my sister? Did it have something to do with me? With how he'd been calling to me?

But I wouldn't get any answers here, so I took a deep breath, did my best to push away my pounding headache, and motioned for the others to follow.

"Let's get going," I said. "The sooner we can get to that cave, the better."

Our shoes shifted over sand as we marched toward the jungle. Fandalore trailed along, noisily chewing on his coconut. He offered me a bite, but I politely refused. I hadn't had an appetite since we'd landed on the island.

When we reached the imposing wall of palm trees blocking us, their long shadows clawed at us as if they were long, grasping talons. Goosebumps formed on my skin.

"Thimblethorn will never fit through those trees," Luria said, glancing back at the dragon.

"No matter," the dragon said. "I shall wait here on the beach for you. When you arrive at the cave, I shall fly to you." He gave a giant yawn that showed all his teeth. "I daresay flying has sapped my strength. I think a brief nap would do me some good."

"All right," I said. "But wait until nightfall before you fly to us, so they won't be able to see you and shoot you down or something. That's the last thing we need."

The dragon bobbed his big head, then curled up on the warm sand.

As soon as we stepped inside the canopy of the jungle, it seemed to swallow us. The overheated air was so hot and sticky, I felt as if I were trying to breathe through a sheet of plastic. Insects buzzed around my ears and stung my neck. The vines and briars grew so thick, the way became impassible, and I was forced to pull Schubert out from the sheath. I cut through a thick vine when he spoke up.

"Using me as a common machete?" he said with a *tsk*. "I thought by now you would've found the Wraith King and been ready to chop off his head. I'm quite prepared for the task. As I've been shut away for most of your journey and unable to contribute a single word to any of your conversations, I've been thinking. And I'll have you know, I'm not a squeamish sword. No, not at all. The sight of blood doesn't alarm me. I'm used to it. Yes, there may have been a time when I shied away from the sight of gore. But no longer. I've got a strong constitution. Ready for any battle. Give me any amount of blood. I won't shy away. Should you need me to lop off the head of any foe, that's what I shall—"

I whacked another vine. Green slimy puss spilled out and coated the blade in its sticky residue.

"Careful there," he shouted. "What is that? Vine goo? Ohh, disgusting! The slime. My goodness gracious, that is horrible. The smell. Just sickening. I daresay I feel like vomiting. You must clean me, *Hero* Brightblade." He put sarcastic emphasis on the word hero. "Or are we going by Simpleton now? These names are so confounding. No matter. Clean me now, I say!"

Ordinarily, I would've ground my teeth and told Schubert to shut up already. But now, I was doing my best to stay alert and focus through the worsening headache. I whacked so many vines I lost count, and after accusing me of deafness, and then neglect for the next ten minutes, he finally quieted as we entered a clearing.

I cleaned the blade with the hem of my shirt, then gratefully stuffed him back into the sheath. The clearing revealed a sky filled with dark, menacing clouds. Thunder rumbled with a drawn-out growl, and lightning crackled.

Voices drifted in the distance.

"I think we're getting close to Bravestone's camp," I whispered to the others. We hid behind a bush and peered through a gap in the leaves. Red tents sat around a clearing, and smoke curled lazily from a fire that was little more than glowing coals. I saw no signs of Bravestone's dragon, making me wonder if it had been too fragile to make the trip.

A few wooden boxes were stacked near the tents, and I recognized some as the boxes that had been holding the camera gear. Raised shouts came from inside one of the tents.

"...kill you for this," someone shouted.

"Not if he kills you first," another voice yelled back.

"You can't force me."

I glanced at the others as we crouched behind a bush. "That must be Bravestone arguing with his manager."

"Yes," Luria agreed. "It sounds like Mr. Moneymaker is forcing Bravestone to confront the Wraith King."

Maharani scratched his head. "But why would he do that?" he asked. "Bravestone's right. He'll just get killed. Why go up against him when you know you'll die?"

It was a good question. It was such a good question I was forced to ask it of myself. "Maybe they think that since they have the true Hero's sword, they'll be able to stop him," I suggested. "And since they've brought all their cameras and everything, they'll at least be able to show Bravestone confronting the Wraith King."

"But what if he fails miserably?" my cousin asked. "What then?"

"They'll edit it," I answered. "Make it look like Bravestone really killed the Wraith King. It will make people feel more comfortable for a while at least."

"But that's terrible." Luria hissed. Her yellow eyes turned livid. "If they pretend to show Bravestone killing the Wraith King when he really didn't, it will put people at ease. They'll all leave their homes and their protective spells thinking they're safe, then they'll all be turned into wraiths. They're making the Wraith King's job easier."

"But President Falcoon will look like he accomplished something," I said. "At least for a little while."

"I agree," my cousin said. "I'll bet the president started panicking once he found out Mayor Wren's bomb was useless. And now that the president knows the Wraith King is trying to harness the power of the cave, I'll bet he thinks there's nothing else he can do except let Bravestone try and destroy him. It's a last-ditch effort."

"And if Bravestone isn't successful and doesn't happen to stop the Wraith King, and the Wraith King manages to harness the cave's magic and turn everyone on the planet into a wraith, then no big deal. We'll all be wraiths and won't know any better."

Luria sat back on her heels, her jaw clenched. "This is madness. It sounds like they're giving in to defeat."

"Maybe," I said. "But at this point, what other choices do they have?"

"Send an army," she demanded. "Drop every weapon they have on the island."

"What army?" I asked. "What weapons? Our people swore off violence a long time ago. We don't need armies if we have peace. We don't need weapons except for flimsy pistols that only scare people and don't do any lasting harm. That's what happens when people forget history, when we forget what evil looks like and call it a fairy tale instead of what it truly is."

"Then we'll be the ones to stop him," Luria said resolutely. "I saw my father and brother get transformed at the hands of that monster. On that day, I swore I would get them back, and I refuse to break a promise." She spoke with such devotion it scared me. "We're going to make the world right again," she continued. "No more believing in half-truths about our past, about Chaos and Chorus. After we defeat the Wraith King, we'll make sure people know what he really stands for, and hopefully make sure that in five-hundred years, people won't forget again."

My cousin and I only stared with slack jaws at one another. From the clearing, the shouting stopped abruptly. Then, Bravestone marched out of a tent flanked by Mr. Moneymaker and several body-guards. Sunlight glinted on the sword he carried—*my* sword, and I had the insane urge to rush from my hiding place and wrestle it away from him.

I fisted my hands instead and forced myself to be calm and think rationally. There was no chance I'd get it from him now, not with all those people surrounding him. I'd have to follow him and wait for him to place it aside if I wanted to get it back, but that was assuming he would be careless enough to leave it unguarded.

Bravestone and his crew turned away from us. A few people grabbed cameras from the wooden crates and followed behind the group.

"Let's follow them," I whispered to the others. "Quietly."

My friends nodded, and we waited for Bravestone's crew to clear out before following them.

Chapter 19
AN INVISIBLE SOLUTION

Thunder rumbled as we maneuvered through the trees and dense bushes. The damp air held the scent of rain, and my clothes stuck uncomfortably to my skin. My heart raced and my stomach felt queasy. Worse, the headache had only grown worse the closer we got to the cave.

Through gaps in the verdant greenery, Bravestone's red cape fluttered every now and then, giving away his position. But even if he hadn't been wearing it, he would have been impossible not to spot. He traveled with half-a-dozen bodyguards and camera crew. The man dressed as Bravestone's wizard also walked with the group. The whole troop made such a ruckus moving through the bush that following them was like tracking a herd of enraged bull dragons.

Bravestone and his manager still snipped at each other, and I hated to admit it, but I may have felt the teeniest drop of pity for Bravestone. I suspected all he'd ever wanted was fame. Battling the Wraith King was never what he'd signed up to do. Now, here he was, tromping through the jungle toward the Wraith King and to his possible death.

Bravestone's group stopped frequently to wipe off their camera lenses or film Bravestone or his wizard behind one backdrop or another. They asked Bravestone questions like, "how are you feeling right now?" Or "what do you think will happen when you encounter the Wraith King?" Or "do you plan to retire after this?"

Mr. Moneymaker had to stop the production several times, telling Bravestone to tilt his chin a little higher or make sure the sword's hilt was visible for this shot. It was all very silly, and hardly seemed like the kind of thing one should do when preparing to confront the evilest being in the entire world.

I wasn't sure I'd rolled my eyes so many times in all my life.

A few fat raindrops pelted my skin as we approached the shore of the lake. The air held an ominous feeling, the sky dark with storm clouds and the occasional flashes of lightning, the rumble of thunder like a warning growl. The lake water looked unusually calm, with only a few raindrops creating ripples over its placid surface.

Bravestone's group walked along the shore until they stopped abruptly. My friends and I scrambled to hide behind a cluster of briar bushes.

"What are they doing?" my cousin whispered.

"I'm not sure," I answered. "Maybe filming again?"

"No," Luria said as she craned her neck. "Their cameras aren't turned on." She gasped as she stood on her tippy-toes and peeked through a gap in the bushes. "There's a wraith. Wait, three wraiths. What are they doing?"

I tried to see what she was seeing, but I couldn't get a view through the dense greenery, so I snuck to the left side of the bushes and peeked around. Three wraiths stood facing Mr. Moneymaker. He was motioning wildly as he spoke, although I couldn't hear his voice over the rumbling thunder.

"Why aren't they attacking?" I asked quietly when Mr. Moneymaker grabbed Bravestone by the arm and thrust him toward the wraiths. I was shocked that Bravestone didn't protest. He walked calmly toward the wraiths with the sword still strapped to his side.

Mr. Moneymaker laughed, said something else, and the wraiths glided away with Bravestone between them. After Bravestone disappeared over a rise and into the thick jungle, Mr. Moneymaker spun on his heel and motioned for the others to make camp.

"Until it happens," I heard him yell.

"What's going on?" I asked as I crouched by my friends once again.

"They just sent Bravestone to die," my cousin answered. "Did you see how Mr. Moneymaker gave him away? There wasn't a fight or anything."

"Something weird is going on," I said. "But I'm not sure what. What did Mr. Moneymaker mean when he said something about *until it happens*. Until *what* happens?"

Luria tapped her finger on her lip. "There's only one way to find out. We'll have to sneak past Bravestone's camp and follow the wraiths who took him."

"That could be really dangerous," Maharani said. "You know that, right?"

"Not if we do this the right way," she said.

"What do you mean?" I asked.

A twinkle lit her eyes as she glanced at her staff. "I'll make our visibility useless."

"You'll make us invisible?" I asked.

"Yes," she answered. "More or less."

"You really think that will work?" my cousin asked.

"I think so," she answered. "I mean, I'm pretty sure."

"*Pretty* sure?" I questioned.

"I've never tried turning someone invisible, so of course I'm not completely sure. But what other choice do we have right now? If we try to follow Bravestone as is, we'll get caught."

My cousin shrugged. "She's right."

"Okay," I said. "Let's try."

Luria nodded, and we stood. Amethyst crystals glowed as Luria held her staff. "Place your hands by mine," she said, and my cousin and I grabbed the wooden shaft, my hands above Luria's and his beneath. "I'm going to whisper the spell," she said in a quiet voice. "Just stay still while I do it." Her usually confident voice held an edge of uncharacteristic doubt, which made a knot of nervousness squeeze my throat.

"Luria," Maharani said. "This isn't permanent, right? You can make us visible again, can't you?"

"Yeah, sure," she answered too quickly. "No problem. I'll just make the invisibility useless whenever we're ready. Easy."

Maharani and I traded uneasy glances. I wasn't buying her assurances, but I didn't question her as she closed her eyes and started whispering words of a spell. The air grew quiet around us. Magic prickled my skin and raised the hairs on my arms and back of my neck. She hummed a few of the words in a melodic voice, one that made the purple crystals glitter brighter. It was a simple tune that held a deep power. Then, with a final whispered word, magic glowed from her hands, then the light flowed from her fingers to ours. As the light faded, it left our fingers invisible.

The glow trailed from our hands to our arms and torsos, shining bright until it faded and left us so translucent, I could only see our forms if we moved.

"It's working," I whispered to Maharani who gave a quick nod before the light surrounded his neck, then his face. Soon, all I could see was a single staff standing as if by its own power. And then, it too disappeared.

"It worked," I heard Luria's voice speak as if from thin air. She spoke with a sigh of relief, as if she hadn't quite believed she'd really be successful. "Can you believe it? It worked."

"This feels so weird," my cousin said. I could just barely see the air shift where he'd been standing as he ran his hands over his arms. "I can still feel my body, but I can't see it. Gordy, try putting your hands in front of your face. Cuz, this is crazy. I can see through my own hands."

"Don't get too excited," Luria chided. "We don't have time to play around. We need to follow Bravestone and figure out why he went with those wraiths. Come on, follow me." She must have turned because I heard her feet crunch over dead leaves on the ground.

"Luria," I hissed, hoping she would stop walking in time to hear me. "Hold on. We can't see where you're going. We need a way to stay together."

"Right," she said. "Just look down." I glanced at the ground where I could see a faint pair of footprints. "Follow my tracks," she said. "Plus, you can see the air shift when we move. Try to focus on one of those."

"Okay," I answered. "But let's just go carefully. If we can see the air shifting, then so can anyone else who's paying attention."

"Good point," my cousin said.

"Stay close," Luria cautioned. A twig snapped as she moved forward. We walked toward Bravestone's camp, although gave them a wide berth as twigs continued snapping underfoot, and small saplings got pushed aside. Anyone looking close enough would have seen us, but thankfully, Mr. Moneymaker and his group sat on logs and spoke quietly to one another.

Even so, nerves pinched my stomach as I took careful steps and kept my eyes on their group. At one point, Mr. Moneymaker stood and paced nearby. We stopped, and I held my breath, but soon, he walked away and grabbed a handful of granola bars from his backpack. The rustling of the wrappers helped mask our footfalls, and we continued until they were far behind us.

We continued through the forest until the trees parted to reveal a clearing. The red dragon lay curled up with his head resting on his tail. His eyes were closed, but I couldn't be sure if he was asleep.

As I glanced at the dragon, I ran into the very solid form of Luria, and I had to do my best not to wince out loud.

"Luria," I hissed as quietly as humanly possible.

"Sorry," she whispered back. "I just wanted to make sure the dragon was sleeping."

One of the dragon's eyes lazily opened, revealing an orange iris that was the shocking reddish-orange hue of blazing fire. My heart stopped. I didn't dare move. Didn't dare breathe.

Don't look this way, don't look this way, I repeated in my head.

Finally, the dragon yawned, then closed his eyes, and I finally found the courage to breathe again.

That was too close, I said to myself, then focused on the path ahead. I carefully followed Luria's footprints. The eerie wails of wraiths came from ahead. As we drew closer, the wails grew louder, and I was forced to remind myself why I was doing this.

They've got my sister, I said to myself. *They'll turn us all into wraiths unless we stop them.*

We stepped out of the forest and into an area filled with black volcanic rocks created from lava flows. The air held the faint scent of brimstone. A towering step-pyramid came into view. Although it was covered in vines, I could still make out the triangular shape.

We approached the pyramid, then took a narrow trail circling the wide base. I looked in awe at the pyramid looming over us. Most of the stones were crumbling and out of place, but a few remained intact, and I could even make out a few symbols carved into the stone.

After making it around the pyramid, we entered an area devoid of plants or greenery of any kind. Not even a weed grew among the broken stones. Some of the rocks were pumice and full of holes, while others resembled sheets of black glass.

Hovering above the rock-strewn ground were at least a hundred wraiths. They hung lifelessly in the air, moaning every now and then, although their eyes were blank, and a tremor of fear spiked through my heart.

The idea of becoming one of them repulsed me, and I renewed my determination to stop the Wraith King at whatever cost. This couldn't be allowed to continue. It didn't matter that they couldn't feel pain. What was the point if they couldn't feel joy either?

I watched the air shift in front of me as we walked around the edge of the crowd of wraiths. It felt as if every set of dead eyes were following me, although when I glanced at them, they only stared with unfocused gazes.

The sound of a cape fluttering in the breeze came from ahead of us, and we rounded a boulder to find Alexander Bravestone standing at the entrance to the cave. Its opening spanned at least two-stories tall.

My heart gave a giant leap of one part excitement and another part fear. Several wraiths hovered around Bravestone, and one of them clutched Bravestone's arm in a tight grasp.

It was hard for me to look at that decaying hand for too long. Although it appeared half-translucent in some places on its wrist and a few fingers, I could still see chunks of dried skin hanging from the hand up to the elbow. Scabs and open sores covered what flesh remained, and I had to take a deep breath of fresh air to chase away the nausea souring my stomach.

This was a person not long ago, I said to myself. *And now look at him.*

"Tell the Wraith King to meet me out here," Bravestone demanded. "I refuse to go in there. He comes to me, or the deal is off."

"Nooo," the wraiths moaned in an eerie, hissing wail, then others flew to him and grabbed his remaining free arm. "You must come. You must go to him," they repeated. They tugged until he was forced to stumble forward and enter the cave. His protests echoed until he walked too far away for us to hear.

The air shifted beside me. I watched Luria's form move as we huddled behind the giant rock. Even though we were invisible, I supposed we all felt safer being behind the shelter of the boulder.

"Why did he want the Wraith King to come out here?" I asked.

"Maybe he felt more comfortable?" my cousin suggested. "Personally, I wouldn't feel safe going inside a creepy cave—especially with the Wraith King inside it."

"There's got to be more to it," Luria said. "Bravestone is up to something. Not sure what yet."

"Do you think we'll have to follow him in there?" my cousin asked.

"I don't think we have a choice," I said. "We've got to get the sword back before Bravestone does something really stupid, like blow himself up along with the Wraith King."

Luria gasped. "Surely he would never agree to a plan like that?"

"It's possible," I said. "It might be why he wanted the Wraith King to come out here, so he could blow up all the wraiths in the process."

"It wouldn't work anyway," Maharani said. "Wraiths can't die. Neither can the Wraith King."

"But Bravestone and his group don't think like that," I offered. "They're still thinking in modern terms. Probably think a bomb would be a great way to kill them all at once."

"No matter what Bravestone's plan is," Luria said. "We've still got to go inside that cave. I haven't seen Val anywhere out here, which means she's most likely inside. We can't just let her die."

I swallowed a nervous lump in my throat as I looked at the cave's dark gaping maw, like the open mouth of a venomous snake just waiting to devour us.

Chapter 20
THE CAVE OF CHAOS

Darkness engulfed us as we walked inside the cave. I wasn't expecting the temperature to drop so drastically, but it soon got so cold that I was shivering. Water dripped rhythmically in the distance. A few rusted sconces held burning torches. The flames only sputtered a little as we passed.

My thoughts went back to the story Chieftain Kalize had told us. Chaos had died here, and Chorus had found him. It was hard to think of being trapped in absolute darkness with nothing to eat or drink. I couldn't imagine a more depressing way to die, so I forced myself to think of something else instead.

The path sloped, and I thought I heard a very faint caw emanating from up ahead. My pulse sped up. Was it Val? Another caw echoed the first, and I knew it had to be her.

Ahead, the tunnel made a sharp curve to the left, and raised voices reverberated from just ahead. Luria's hand grabbed mine, and I heard a whispered shush close to my ear. "Wait here."

My cousin bumped into my arm, and I grabbed it. "We're waiting here," I told him, and I heard a faint "okay" in response.

As I peeked around the corner, a cavernous, domed room supported by carved pillars came into view. Across the vast space, the pleading voice came from Bravestone who stood opposite a stone pedestal. On the other side of him stood a sight I could barely register.

Val lay tied to the pedestal, her black, feathered body circled in ropes that pinned her to the stone surface.

The Wraith King stood over her.

The fear I'd gotten from seeing the pictures in the books and in my nightmares were nothing compared to this. Dread washed over me and froze me to the spot. I realized I was clutching Schubert's pommel so tightly, my knuckles hurt, and I could only imagine his protests at being so horribly handled.

But I didn't dare move, didn't dare breathe. Although his red eyes were focused on Bravestone, I still felt as if he knew I was here, invisible or not. Still, perhaps I had a small element of surprise on my side, as the Wraith King was too focused on Bravestone to pay attention to me.

"He's still wearing the sword," my cousin pointed out.

"Yes," Luria said. "One of us might be able to sneak up and take it out of the sheath while he's distracted."

"I can do it," my cousin offered.

"No," Luria disagreed. "No offense, Maharani. But you're not the fastest or the quietest. Let me do it. I've got experience sneaking around."

"No," I said resolutely. "I've got to do it." I spoke with firmness, although I felt nothing but complete terror. "It's my sword. My quest. My responsibility." I took a deep breath to try and calm down. "I'll do it."

"Are you sure?" my cousin asked.

"Yes," I answered. "That's my sister on the pedestal. I'll pull out the sword from Bravestone's sheath and stab the Wraith King before he has a chance to react, then I'll cut my sister free, and we can escape." I doubted it would be that easy, but I couldn't overthink my idea or I'd chicken out and never do it.

I snuck away from the wall where my friends were hiding and headed toward the pedestal. Several wraiths hovered around the chamber. Some floated closer to the ceiling, others near the ground. Only their robes moved in a phantom wind as they stood watching Bravestone face the Wraith King.

I hadn't paid much attention to Bravestone until now, but as I drew closer, his words drifted across the cavern toward me, growing more audible as I approached.

"...have to go outside for this," he demanded. "What's the big deal anyway?"

The Wraith King didn't speak. He only placed his hand over my sister's body. The sight of his clawed fingers touching my sister was enough to make a fist of rage punch my chest.

"You can have your stupid sword if you go outside," Bravestone continued. "Isn't that what you want? Why are you just standing there like a dumb idiot? Why aren't you listening to me?"

The Wraith King's laugh was enough to set my teeth on edge. It was such an unnatural, grating sound and devoid of humanity.

"You, child," he said finally, "have no authority here."

Bravestone grabbed the sword's hilt, but he didn't remove it. "You're wrong. I've got the Hero's sword, and that gives me all the authority I need. You can't do anything without this sword."

The Wraith King didn't respond. He only stood there with his clawed hand covering my sister's body, as if waiting for something.

What if he's waiting for me? I thought to myself, then squashed the idea. No. I couldn't let myself think that way. Even if it were true, then what? I turned around and ran away and never looked back?

I'd already come this far. I was too close to my sister. Too close to stopping the Wraith King and saving everyone on the planet. I wouldn't leave unless she was safe. If the Wraith King happened to kill me? Then...

I took a deep breath as intense fear spread like ice through my veins. I'd never really thought of my own death until now. But what happened if I died? If I went to the spirit realm, how long would I have to wait for my family to join me? I'd never actually pondered death. Casually, sure. Sometimes we'd gathered as a family and studied the stories of Chorus. We'd sang the hymns of how we would reunite in the next world, in a place more beautiful than we could comprehend.

But those had been stories too far removed for me to grasp. But now...

Death, I thought. Was I really prepared for it?

Bravestone's cries for the Wraith King to leave the cave grew more insistent, making me realize the cameras would most likely be set up out there so they could get the best shots of Bravestone confronting the Wraith King.

I could just imagine Mr. Moneymaker now. *It's better lighting. More room to move around. We won't be able to see a thing in the cave. Just bring him out here, stab him, and this whole episode will be over, and we can all go home. Isn't that what you want?*

Home. The word tugged at my heartstrings so powerfully, I was forced to blink away the tears prickling my eyes. More than anything I just wanted to go home. Yes, at one time I'd thought adventuring was my only goal in life. But now, I would give anything just to sit with Mom, Dad, and Kyrie around the dinner table, laughing about something silly our fairies had done.

I took a step forward and then another. My heart pounded so fast all I could hear was the blood whooshing through my ears. My hands had grown so clammy as I gripped Schubert's pommel, I wasn't sure I would be able to remove it if I needed to—not that I was planning to remove Schubert.

No, for this plan to work, I'd have to sneak up behind Bravestone and remove the real sword from him. Bravestone kept ranting as I crept behind him, his red cape flying wildly as he motioned to the corridor behind us.

I focused on the tarnished silver pommel sticking out from the sheath at his side, but when I grabbed for it, he took a step forward.

Stay still. I wanted to yell as I ground my teeth and grabbed for it again. This time, I got a good grip on it and yanked it out before he could move.

As soon as the sword rose into the air—seemingly by itself—Bravestone stopped ranting. He looked with shock at the sword hovering beside him.

"What—?" he started to say when I ran straight for the Wraith King. But instead of stabbing him, the Wraith King's form vanished. The sword passed through thin air, throwing me off balance. I fell forward. With my hands already slick with sweat, the sword flew from my grasp and scuttled over the stone floor.

The Wraith King reappeared. He stood over the sword, a wicked gleam in his ruby eyes as he picked it up with his clawed hands. Irrational terror spread through my insides and froze me to the stone floor.

He'd known I was coming. He'd known I was coming all along. He'd planned this.

The Wraith King didn't hesitate to speed straight for Bravestone. He moved so fast, all I could see was a blur of his tall form and gleaming silver armor, wearing the skull of his own father. He struck Bravestone, and the boy fell back, screaming.

The Wraith King ripped the sword from Bravestone's body. The boy clutched his midsection, his eyes wide with pain and complete shock. "You... you..." he gasped, as if he couldn't believe the Wraith King would actually harm him.

Are you really that stupid? I wanted to scream at him. *He's not just some man in a costume. He's the Wraith King!*

The Wraith King waved his hand, and a dense cloud of gray fog surrounded the boy. Bravestone gasped. His face drained of color, and his clothes turned the same gray as the fog. The pristine material of his questing gear, including his red cloak, morphed into tatty rags. The Wraith King took another step forward and grabbed Bravestone's face between his bony, claw-tipped fingers.

"Enjoy these last moments," he hissed. "Let terror be your final emotion... Remember it... Fear. Pain."

Bravestone gasped, then choked. His face changed to ashy gray. His once vivid eyes drained of life until they were a dull silver with only a slight hint of lingering blue. I'd never seen anyone transformed into a wraith before. I'd seen wraiths, sure. But watching the actual transformation was so unnatural, repulsion welled up inside me and sickened me.

"You're one of mine now," the Wraith King said in his cold, emotionless voice. "Now you will know true freedom. Freedom from emotion and pain. Freedom from worry. Freedom from death. Go." He raised his hand and pointed at the other wraiths gathered behind them. "Be with your brothers and sisters."

The wraith glided away without protesting, its robes gliding and fanning out in a phantom wind.

"Yes, Gordy," the Wraith King said, his back still turned as he gripped the sword with Bravestone's blood on it. "That's what you'll become. Soon. Very soon."

The shock at his words, and especially that he knew my name, was enough to make an iron spike of fear stab my heart. But I refused to let him scare me. He'd done enough of that already.

"No," I forced as much bravery into my voice that I could muster.

"No?" He spun around, a half-smile tugging at his lips. Up close, I realized he didn't look like one of the wraiths. For one thing, his flesh was still whole and intact, his face covered in a pattern of red and black scales. Also, his clothing wasn't the tatty robes of a wraith, but armor, with a silver breastplate and greaves, and black leather armor beneath.

For another thing, his smile told me he still had emotions, unlike the wraiths he controlled. He strode a step closer to me, and fear made my heart hammer in my chest. With a wave of his hand, a gray mist engulfed my body, and my skin prickled as if I'd been electrified. I lifted my hands only to see them become visible.

"Yes," he said, pacing around me. "I've been watching you with interest since you obtained the Hero's sword. I thought I'd destroyed all the Chosen when I reawakened. The idea that I'd missed someone was absurd. I knew you were never a Chosen." His eyes flared as if flames danced in his red pupils. "But your ability to claim the Hero's sword was of interest to me. I debated on killing you after you first removed it, but I resisted. Better to let the little fool bring the sword here, straight to me." He lifted the blade, and a wicked grin stretched his mouth. "You're probably not aware of this, but the Hero's sword is the only weapon capable of unleashing Chorus's magic. You'll be part of this, *Shia'va*. As will your family." He paced back to the crow pinned to the pedestal, and I rushed toward her.

No! I wouldn't let him hurt my sister. Heart pounding, I stood over the pedestal. The crow looked pleadingly up at me, her eyes wide with fear. Her chest rose and fell with her rapid, panting breaths.

I shielded the bird with my arms. "Don't touch her," I said through clenched teeth. "Don't come a step closer."

His laugh grated in my ears. "You misunderstand my intentions." He moved his hand in a slashing motion, and the ropes pinning her to the pedestal disappeared. Shocked, I lifted my arms, and she used her wings for balance to hobble onto her feet.

"Don't you see?" the Wraith King said. "I'm here to bring equality to the world. It's been my life's mission since I was born. You've been taught I'm evil, yes. But is equality evil? Is ending suffering and pain evil? Is restoring order evil? Is this evil?" He waved his hand again, and the familiar gray fog clouded around my sister. At first, I panicked, thinking he was turning her into a wraith just like he'd done to Bravestone.

But as I watched the crow transform, she morphed from a crow back to a girl, with blonde ringlets and tired but smiling eyes. She collapsed on the pedestal, her frame smaller and frailer than I remembered.

"You changed her back?" I asked, awe and confusion warring within me.

"Yes," he said. "It's my payment to you for delivering this to me." He raised the Hero's sword.

"I didn't bring it here," I snapped. "Bravestone did."

"I disagree," he said with a slight smile. "You removed it from the dungeon. You unsheathed it when you arrived here. You practically handed it to me. Who am I to question your intentions with the sword?"

"My intentions were to kill you with it," I growled.

"*Kill* me?" He loomed close enough for me to see orange flecks in his scarlet pupils. "You of all people should know I can't die." He took a step away from me. "Now, I suppose you're wondering why I've transformed your sister." At his words, I grabbed my sister's hand. Her fingers were shockingly cold and so thin I thought they might break.

"Gordy," she whispered to me, her lips pale and shivering.

"Kyrie," I whispered back and gave her hand a gentle squeeze.

"I have a proposition for you," the Wraith King said.

"A proposition?" I questioned.

"Yes. You see, shortly after discovering the whereabouts of this cave, I located the source of its magic." He waved behind him, and an arch of glowing magic appeared where the stone wall had been. Magical runes also glowed along the edges of the archway. I felt the prickle of its power from here. The spell was so strong, a cold shiver ran down my spine.

The Wraith King's armor reflected the gateway's blue glow as he motioned to it. "Chorus's magic resides just beyond this doorway. But only a flesh and blood being can obtain its power—a being who is pure of heart and selfless in nature." He paced to the glowing archway, then stretched his hand toward it. A bolt of white-hot lightning blasted his hand. I could feel its searing heat from here.

A blackened mark cut the palm of his hand, although he didn't wince as I would've expected a normal person to do.

"You completed the trials of Chorus to remove the Hero's sword from the dungeon beneath the Elderhurst ruins. That same magic resides inside the chamber beyond this gateway. I need you to go inside to obtain the magic for me. That's all I ask."

"That's all?" I asked mockingly.

"You'll be rewarded," he added, then motioned to my sister. "I've seen your heart. I know your greatest desire."

"Really?" I challenged. "I doubt it."

"I understand there are those who desire to remain as they are without becoming one of mine, which is the reward you will receive if you do as I ask. You shall remain in your human form, as will your sister." His booted footsteps echoed through the dome of the cavern as he paced around me. "You've already seen I have the ability to transform her to her true form. I can do the same for your family. Your friends." He moved his hand in a wavelike pattern, and gray mist gathered around him. The pressure of magic weighed heavily, like I'd been submerged deep underwater. As the fog engulfed the room, familiar voices rang out. Could it be?

"Mom?" I asked, the fog muffling my voice. "Dad?"

"Gordy," Mom said with relief in her voice.

"Is that you?" Dad echoed her.

"It's me! I'm here!" I wasn't sure I'd ever felt as much relief as I felt in that moment. As the fog lifted, the silhouettes of my mom and dad came into view. I ran to them, and they hugged me in a tight embrace. The scent of dish soap lingered on Mom's hands, and Dad's strong fingers gripped my shoulders.

Tears prickled my eyes. "I missed you so *so* much."

"Mom?" Kyrie's small voice called from the pedestal. "Dad?"

"Kyrie," my parents said in unison, then they rushed to her and grabbed her up. Dad cradled her in his big arms, his red beard tickling her forehead as he held her to his chest. I didn't care that we were in a cave with the most demonic creature in the world, being with my family pushed away all my doubts and fears. I only wished we could've been together at home. But no, the Wraith King had brought them here. But, why?

As if sensing my thoughts, he approached us. "You see, Gordy. I can make them safe. You can live here on this island away from the rest of us. You'll be protected. As will your friends." Once again, he motioned with his arm toward the corner where my friends had been hiding.

As their forms became visible, Maharani raised his hands to his face. His mouth fell open in a shocked expression, although Luria only stood there looking daggers at the Wraith King.

"You can all be here, Gordy. Safe and unharmed. All you need to do is enter through the gateway and bring me the magic." He spoke in a soft tone, one meant to put me at ease.

A million thoughts spiraled through my head so quickly, I became dizzy. What an impossible decision. The selfish part of me wanted to say yes. Wouldn't it be so much easier to go get the magic and be done with the Wraith King for good? All the important people in my life would be saved. We could forget any of this had ever happened and just live our lives as normal.

But what about Uncle Harlowe? What about Luria's brother and dad? What about Chieftain Kalize and his clan? What about everyone on the entire planet?

"No," I said firmly. "I won't do it."

"No?" He tilted his head. "Well, I daresay, I'm not surprised. When you've seen as much as I have, you learn patterns in people. People like you, Gordy. Children who think they can be heroes simply by being Chosen. Yes, I know your type. I know your thoughts and decisions even before you make them."

His words affected me more than I wanted to let on. I'd always had an irrational fear that the Wraith King knew me. He'd come to me in my dreams too many times to discount the feeling.

But what if he was lying?

Maybe he knew my type. Maybe he'd known others like me. But how could he possibly know me?

"With that in mind," he continued. "I can see what motivates you." His snakelike eyes flicked to my family. "Should you choose to refuse me, your family shall be the first to become wraiths."

My stomach bottomed out, and now I knew the real reason the Wraith King had brought them here. Not to help them, but to use them.

The Wraith King lifted his hand, and the gray fog engulfed them.

"No," I screamed.

The Wraith King held his hand steady, and the fog stopped swirling. My family stood frozen within the dense mist, as if they were statues. My mother's face was etched with shock. Dad still cradled Kyrie to his chest and didn't look up, and Kyrie hugged him as if she would never let go.

Could I really doom them to become wraiths? Maybe I couldn't save everyone. Maybe I was never meant to save everyone. If I was only meant to save my family, then that's what I would do.

"Fine," I ground out. "I'll do it. I'll get the magic for you. But if you even look at my family or my friends, I'll destroy the magic for good. You'll never get a chance to use it."

Eyes twinkling with a glint of satisfaction, he gave a single nod, then motioned over his shoulder. "Bring the magic to me. That's all I ask."

With a trickle of fear racing down my spine, I stepped toward the glowing archway. *For my family,* I said under my breath.

Chapter 21
THE SPHERE

*S*top, a voice yelled in my head. *Don't do it. Don't give him the magic.*

The archway's azure glow shone over me. My skin prickled everywhere the light touched. I stood at the entryway. It looked taller from this angle. Runes glowed with such intensity I couldn't look at them for too long without burning my retinas.

I reached for the doorway, but hesitated, then glanced over my shoulder. My family still stood frozen in the gray mist, but beyond them stood Luria and Maharani. I gave them a pleading glance. I knew they would surely hate me forever for what I was about to do. But wasn't it better to save a few people than no one?

They looked at me with wide, fearful eyes.

My heart tugged with guilt so badly, I was forced to turn away from them. Even so, all I could see were their grief-stricken faces. I was about to doom their families to live as wraiths for the rest of eternity, and I couldn't think of a single way to stop it from happening.

But if I didn't do this, *everyone* would become a wraith. At least this way we'd still have a fighting chance. A few of us would survive, and maybe in the future we'd get a chance to stop the Wraith King once again. Right?

Yes, I told myself. *Focus on that. Another chance. Another day.* But no, it wasn't good enough. I refused to just give in to the Wraith King's demands. I had to do something—*anything*—to stop him.

As I stood at the doorway, I wasn't sure how to open it, so I decided on placing my hand against the stones. The light grew brighter, and I got the feeling it was searching me, determining if I was worthy of entering. The cold chilled my palm, but soon, the blue light turned golden, then, the stones disappeared.

A dark tunnel stretched in front of me.

Do something, a voice screamed in my head. *Don't just go in there and get the magic.*

I spun around and faced the Wraith King who still stood by the pedestal. "It's too dark in there," I said, hedging for any excuse I could. "I won't be able to see how to get the magic. I need my friends to come with me." I pointed to Luria and Maharani. "Luria's got a staff that lights up. And Maharani has a shield in case we need protection against anything that tries to kill us."

The Wraith King's eyes narrowed. He didn't speak. He only nodded and gave a wave of his hand in a dismissive gesture, as if my friends were nothing to him and not worth his time. I could almost imagine what he was thinking: If I brought him the magic, he didn't care who helped.

"Come on," I said to my friends, and they rushed past my still-frozen family and past the Wraith King. He didn't even look at them as they hurried to reach my side.

"Inside," I murmured quickly and ushered them into the tunnel. We stepped into the darkness. Behind us, the open doorway we'd stepped through sealed close with a quiet hissing of magic. The purple crystals of Luria's staff illuminated the stones surrounding us.

"Gordy." Luria spoke insistently. "What are you doing? You can't give him the magic."

"I know," I countered. "But don't worry. I have a plan."

"You do?" Maharani questioned hesitantly.

"Yeah." I cleared my throat. "Umm... sort of."

"You *don't* have a plan," Luria said with a disappointed sigh.

"No." I rubbed my neck, realizing the pounding headache I'd had for so long was suddenly gone. Interesting. "Look," I said. "My headache is gone. I think that means the Wraith King can't track me in here, which hopefully means he can't hear us, either."

"Which gives us time to plan... something," Maharani said.

"Yeah," I said. "Something."

"Whatever we plan," Luria said darkly, "in no way can you give in to his demands and just give him the magic. My family are still wraiths, Gordy," she said pleadingly. "And Maharani's dad isn't safe either, and neither is anyone else in the entire world. Just because he's saving your family—*supposedly*—doesn't mean he's saving ours."

"I know," I repeated with a little more heat in my voice than I intended. "Believe me, I get it. Just let me think."

"While you're thinking," my cousin said. "How about let's get through this tunnel." He rubbed his hands over his arms. "This place makes me feel claustrophobic."

"Yeah," I answered. "Let's do that."

Luria's staff gave us light as we walked through the narrow tunnel. With my headache gone, I felt as if I could finally think. Surely there was some way for us to save everyone and not just my family. But how?

"We have to stab the Wraith King with the Hero's sword," I said. "That's the only way to stop him for good."

"But he's got the sword," Maharani said.

"Yeah." My shoulders fell. "And I have no idea how to get it back."

We entered a large chamber that had a domed ceiling. At its center was a pedestal like the one where the Wraith King had tied my sister, except this platform held a glowing ball of lightning blue magic.

"That's it," I said in a hushed, reverent voice. "Chorus's magic must be contained in that sphere."

Our footsteps echoed through the room as we crossed toward the podium. The sphere's light bobbled and waved as it shone around the room, as if we were underwater. Inside the transparent sphere, azure blue magic flowed like molten lava.

Its intensity made my heart beat so rapidly, I had to take a deep breath to keep my cool. I'd never felt a pressure so powerful. The crushing sensation was so strong, I felt as if I were stuck on the bottom of an ocean submerged under trillions of tons of water.

"Do I just take it?" I asked as I stood over the sphere.

"I don't know," my cousin said. "What if it shoots lightning at you or something?"

"Or what if I have to trade something to get it?" I suggested. "Like I had to do for the sword."

"I doubt it," Luria said. "You already proved your worth by getting the sword, which is the only reason the magic allowed you to come inside."

I reached forward and gingerly touched the sphere. When nothing happened, I grabbed it, half expecting the room to start shaking or the room to collapse. "I got it," I said. "I can't believe it was that easy."

"I wouldn't get too excited just yet," Luria cautioned. "Now we've got to figure out how to keep it away from the Wraith King."

"Maybe I should put it back," I said, staring at the swirling magic inside the sphere. The glowing, twisting bands of power mesmerized me, and the idea of handing it over to the Wraith King repulsed me. "Just leave it here and tell the Wraith King I couldn't get it."

"Then he'll just turn us into wraiths like he did to Bravestone," my cousin said morosely. "He won't have any use for us anymore."

"If only we could think of a way to trick him," Luria said. "It wouldn't have to be a big distraction. Just something small enough to interrupt him for a second so we can take the Hero's sword and stab him with it."

My cousin pulled the shield off his back and propped it against his legs. "This thing is so heavy," he said, rubbing his shoulders. The shield's shiny surface reflected the image of me holding the glowing sphere. An idea came to me.

"Luria," I said. "Would it be possible for you to create a fake sphere? One we could trick the Wraith King with?"

"Maybe," she answered hesitantly. "But he'd know it wasn't real."

"That's okay," I said. "It only needs to fool him for a second or two, just long enough for one of us to grab the sword and stab him with it."

"All right," she said. "I can try. But what will we do with the real sphere?"

"Make it look like something else," Maharani suggested. "A pouch or something." He reached into his cloak and pulled out a leather satchel with drawstring ties on the top. As he hefted it, something crunched. "It's just got a bunch of old peanut shells inside. But..." his face lit up. "What if we make the sphere and satchel trade places? We make the sphere look like this pouch..."

"And the pouch look like the sphere," I finished for him as I followed along with his line of thinking. "Maharani, you're genius."

"Thanks," he muttered, blushing.

"Luria, do you think you can transform them?" I asked.

"Maybe." She tapped a finger on her lips as she concentrated on the sphere. "Technically, I'll be making the sphere look useless. And since the food pouch will only look like the sphere and not have its actual powers, it will also technically be useless, too." She took a deep breath and stepped to the sphere. "I've never used magic on something so powerful before. This could backfire horribly."

"But we've got to try," I said. "And we need to do it quickly before the Wraith King gets suspicious that we're up to something."

Luria bit her lip and gave a single nod. "All right," she said in a nervous, breathy voice. "I'll try it. But I can't guarantee this will work. I have no idea how my magic will react to the sphere. I could end up blowing us up or something. But..." she squared her shoulders. "Seeing how our current choices are extremely limited, I guess that's a risk we'll have to take."

She held her staff for a moment without moving. Purple crystals glittered, accentuating the fear in her catlike yellow eyes. Then, she took a deep breath and stepped toward me.

"You've got this," I told her gently.

She gave me a strained smile. "I hope so," she whispered before closing her eyes. She moved her staff in a swirling motion over the sphere, then spoke in a musical whisper. The cavern reverberated with the sound of her voice. The rhythmic cadence of her words echoed through the domed space as if we stood in a cathedral. A purple mist surrounded the sphere, then it moved to surround Maharani's satchel. When the fog cleared, I held a satchel that was an exact match to my cousin's, and he held a sphere that looked exactly like the one I'd held only a moment ago.

"Perfect," I said.

"Let's trade," my cousin said, and I nodded as we switched. He took the transformed sphere, which now looked like his pouch, and stuffed it in his cloak's pocket. I held the satchel which now looked like the sphere, although it weighed much lighter than the actual one. It must have weighed just as much as the pouch, and the feeling I'd had while being near it—of feeling like I was being crushed under the pressure of millions of gallons of water—started to dissipate.

Taking a deep breath, I cupped the fake sphere in my hands. "Okay," I said. "Let's do this. When I give this to the Wraith King, he'll use the sword the sword to break open the sphere and unleash its magic. When it doesn't work, he'll know it's fake. That only gives us a limited time to remove the sword and stab the Wraith King."

"But who's going to do it?" my cousin asked. "If you're the one who gives him the sphere, that leaves me or Luria." He traded glances with Luria. "But... neither of us are the Chosen One. Shouldn't you be the one to do it, Gordy?"

"No," I said. Although I tried to hide it, disappointment was evident in my voice. "We all know I'm not the Chosen One. And really... it doesn't matter who stabs the Wraith King so long as it gets done, right?"

"But that's not true," my cousin argued. "Gordy, you're the one who came up with the plan to be the Chosen One. You're the one who convinced Thimblethorn and Fandalore to go on this quest with us. You're the one who got the Hero's sword from the dungeon. Isn't it obvious? You're the hero."

"But—" I started to argue when Luria spoke up.

"Maharani's right," she said. "You're the one who had all the nightmares about the Wraith King. He calls you Shia'va for a reason. What if you really are the Chosen One?"

"No," I said. "My grandpa told me I wasn't, so I'm not."

"But what if he was wrong?" my cousin questioned.

An unexpected surge of excitement swelled in my chest. I'd spent so long convincing myself that I couldn't be the Chosen One, when deep down, it was all I'd ever wanted. I'd spent hours poring over every book about the past Chosen. There was a time I would've given anything to trade places with Kaladin the Brave standing tall by his throne chair while he held the true Hero's sword—the sword I'd managed to take from the dungeon.

I hadn't stolen it like Bravestone. No. I'd traded for it fair and square. In truth, it had chosen me. Surely that counted just as much as Kaladin or Seann or any of the other Chosen.

If it was truly my one wish in life, then what was stopping me from having it?

"We'll see how it plays out," I said. "When I hand the sphere to the Wraith King, whoever has the best position to take the sword and stab him with it should do it. Doesn't matter who."

They both gave me hesitant looks, as if they'd been waiting for me to say *yes! I've known all along that I'm the Chosen One! I'll defeat the Wraith King or die trying and no one can stop me!* It was most likely what a true Chosen One would've said. But all I said was "let's go."

I cradled the fake orb as we marched for the exit. To the Wraith King. To triumph. Or to our deaths.

Chapter 22
SCHUBERT'S SACRIFICE

The Wraith King's eyes glittered with greed as I held out the orb of Chorus's magic. It still weighed as little as the bag of peanut shells, and I hoped the Wraith King didn't notice. Since he had never held it before, he'd have no reason to question its authenticity. At least, I hoped.

When he took it from me, his claw-tipped fingers looked unnatural against the light of Chorus's supposed magic. Silvery blue bands lit his face in the magical glow.

"Finally," the Wraith King said, holding it over the top of the pedestal. "After hundreds of years. After so much failure. The world will finally know the true meaning of equality. No more death. No more pain. No suffering ever again."

I was shocked to see tears misting his eyes. It struck me that he truly thought he was doing the right thing. I almost felt sorry for him. Almost. But he'd allowed himself to think this way. No one had forced him. He'd become so twisted and perverse that he thought something as evil as taking away a person's soul was a noble cause.

He carefully placed the sphere on top of the platform. Just beyond the pedestal, my family stood frozen in the mist, their eyes wide, their faces filled with shock. I balled my hands into fists as the Wraith King removed the Hero's sword from the sheath at his waist. He started chanting a spell that made my skin turn cold.

"Tu la'via kiavan. Ufa'vi a kin a la. Alu leah Chaos. Baal'am Chorus. Shia'va Chorus." He repeated the phrases over and over until my head felt dizzy. His words grew louder with every sentence he uttered. As he continued, a wind spiraled through the room. Its roar echoed the Wraith King's words.

Still chanting, the Wraith King raised the sword over the sphere. The blade reflected the sphere's light. I wasn't sure my heart had ever pumped so frantically. Luria shifted beside me, and Maharani took a deep breath.

"Be ready," I whispered under my breath to my friends. Luria shocked me when she grabbed my hand and gave it a gentle squeeze. With Maharani and Luria standing on either side of me, I reminded myself that I wasn't alone. They were here with me. Without them, I would have never made it this far.

I gave Luria's hand a gentle squeeze back, praying the fake magical orb would fluster the Wraith King just long enough for one of us to grab the Hero's sword and stab him with it.

The Wraith King lifted the blade high over the sphere. He had the look of a maniac, a twisted smile on his face, as if he were an executioner about to behead his greatest foe. He slammed the blade down.

The orb failed to shatter as one might imagine—with the sound of breaking glass and spiraling bands of brilliant light. Instead, the sound of crunching peanut shells came from the pedestal. The orb transformed back to its original shape. An ordinary bag of busted peanut shells laid on the stone surface. The wind died away, and the cavern became eerily silent.

The Wraith King's face filled with shock, followed by rage. "What?" he yelled so loud that the vibration rattled the small pebbles littering the cave's ground. "Where is it? Where!"

He spun around, eyes livid with unrestrained rage.

"Now," I shouted to my friends. Maharani held his shield in front of the three of us, and we charged toward the Wraith King. We barreled into him so fast, he fell backward, and the sword flew from his grasp. It clattered inches from Luria's feet.

"Luria, now," I shouted. "Grab the sword."

She lunged for the weapon, but the Wraith King was already back on his feet. He grabbed the sword in one swift motion before Luria could reach it. A dozen wraiths cried with ear-shattering wails as they descended on us. Luria shouted a spell, and her staff glowed with a blinding amethyst light. A dense fog of purple mist clouded the cavern.

I choked as the smoke entered my lungs. Chaos descended around us. In the gaps in the mist, wraiths swirled around me. Their mouths opened wide as they screamed with piercing, bone-chilling howls.

One of them flew at me, and I unsheathed Schubert. My blade wouldn't be much use against an undead creature. Maybe if I could hit the bits of solid flesh, it would stun the creature long enough for me to escape. I stabbed the wraith's chest and my blade connected with a rib bone. The wraith flew backward, but only for a moment.

"Find it," the Wraith King yelled. "Find the sphere. One of them must have it. Capture them!"

More wraiths descended on me. I stabbed wildly, managing to nick a chin, then another chest, stunning them as I went. Blindly I stumbled forward, stabbing and flailing with every step. My thoughts turned frantic. Where was my family? Where were my friends? I had to find them before I could escape, but the purple mist made it impossible to see anything but a few inches in front of me.

One of the wraiths dove at me. I stabbed at it, but it dodged, grabbed the blade between its rotting hands, and ripped the sword from my grasp. My weapon clattered onto the stone-strewn ground as it got tossed away. Frigid, bony hands snatched my arms. Sharp fingernails dug into my flesh as three wraiths dragged me to the pedestal.

Mist wafted around Luria and Maharani who were also being held by wraiths beside the pedestal. Behind them, I could just barely make out the silhouettes of my motionless family.

The Wraith King approached me. His scorching, crimson eyes bored into mine, burning with such livid anger I was surprised he didn't catch fire. I'd never felt so much hate radiating from one person.

With both hands, the Wraith King grabbed my neck. His claw-tipped fingers dug into my flesh as he choked me. A cold wave of terror washed over me.

"Where. Is. It?" he demanded, squeezing tighter with every clipped word. My lungs screamed for air. Dots danced in my vision. Did he really expect me to answer while he was choking the life out of me? I gasped and struggled to breathe, but his vice-like grip made it impossible to draw in even the least bit of air.

"Stop... please," I managed.

He's killing me, I thought. *I'm going to die...*

Nothing in my life had prepared me for this moment. I knew then that I wasn't ready for death. A heavy wave of terror engulfed me as the world went black. If I died, at least I knew I'd given my life trying to save everyone.

"Here." My cousin's desperate voice screamed from behind the Wraith King. "It's here. I've got the sphere. Just don't kill Gordy!"

The Wraith King released his chokehold on me and spun around to face Maharani. My cousin held the glowing blue orb in his shaking hands. His face was so pale, it looked as if all the blood had drained from it.

"Take it," he said in a trembling voice, thrusting the orb toward the Wraith King. "Just leave him alone."

The Wraith King gave me a sidelong smirk. He strode forward and snatched the real orb from my cousin's outstretched hands. "Now, the time for uniting every person in our world has arrived. War and death will soon be eradicated forever."

He stood behind the pedestal once again. The silver-blue glow of the true orb gave his face a gray pallor, and he didn't look much different from the wraiths hovering around him.

"Where is the sword?" he demanded of his wraiths, and one of them grabbed the weapon off the ground and handed it to him. A blue sheen flickered from its eyes in a burst so brief, I wouldn't have noticed it if I hadn't been looking.

As the Wraith King stood over the real orb with the sword in hand, dread threatened to make my heart stop beating. His chanted words filled the cavern once again.

"Tu la'via kiavan. Ufa'vi a kin a la…"

This couldn't be happening. We'd been so close to stopping him for him to win now. Wraiths swirled around their king as his chants grew louder.

Alu leah Chaos. Baal'am Chorus. Shia'va Chorus."

The wraiths holding our arms let go to join the mass of other wraiths flying around the king, and an insane idea flashed through my head. I had to take a deep breath to make sure I was thinking clearly, praying my list-ditch effort would work. I whispered the plan to my friends, and they both gave me hesitant looks.

"Trust me," I reassured them.

"Too dangerous," my cousin whispered back.

"We have to try anyway," I said, although my voice was drowned out by the howling wind. "This is our only choice."

"I agree," Luria said with a solemn nod, and Maharani finally nodded, too. Maybe he realized we were about to all be turned to wraiths. If we didn't do this now, we'd never get another chance.

Luria and my cousin quietly followed me as I edged closer to the Wraith King. When my toe caught the edge of a sword on the ground, I froze.

"I found it," I whispered to them.

The Wraith King's words had grown to a fever pitch, but the blood pounding in my ears made it impossible to hear him. Damp mist chilled my fingers as I quickly reached down and grabbed the sword's pommel.

"Luria, Maharani," I whispered to my friends. "We do this together. All three of us. Grab the pommel with me."

My cousin and Luria nodded, and I felt their hands grip the pommel alongside mine. Their hands gave me strength as the fog swirled thicker.

"*Alu leah Chaos,*" the Wraith King yelled. "*Baal'am Chorus. Shia'va Chorus.*"

Wraiths crowded around the raised sword. Their howling mingled with the wind as we edged our way directly behind the Wraith King. His cloak billowed as he raised the sword high overhead, then sliced it downward in one swift motion. The blade struck the orb, but it didn't crack.

At the same time, Luria, Maharani, and I thrust the true Hero's blade into the Wraith King's back.

When the orb didn't shatter, and when the Wraith King fell to his knees, the sword's pommel protruding from his back, I knew we'd won.

The Wraith King shrieked and spun on us, still grasping a sword in his hands with the tip of another sticking from his chest.

"Well done," Schubert yelled at us from the Wraith King's hands. "We've done it, young heroes! I always knew it. I always knew we would—" The Wraith King screamed and threw Schubert across the room with a heave so fierce and full of explosive rage, Schubert's blade shattered into pieces.

"You," the Wraith King snarled with a gurgling choke. "Three. Chosen Ones."

"Chosen *three*, yes," I shouted back at him. "That's right. There was never a chosen one this time, you moron! There were a Chosen Three. And we've stopped you. You'll never turn a single soul into a wraith ever again. You're finished."

For the first time in my life, I finally spoke like a true Chosen.

Magical ice crackled around the Wraith King's feet, solidifying him in place. His skin turned the color of arctic ice. His eyes widened, and his mouth stopped moving, frozen in a soundless scream. As the enchanted ice touched the metal of the blade, the sword slid from the Wraith King's back and hit the stone ground with an echoing clatter. I grabbed it and darted away just as the ice entombed the Wraith King.

All around us, the shrieks of the wraiths died away and changed to shouts of joy. Undead creatures morphed back into their physical forms. Tatty robes became clothing in bright-colored fabrics. Rotting flesh healed and became whole. Dead, listless faces transformed, and tears of joy misted their tired, smiling eyes.

"Dad, Rhys," Luria shouted and ran to a Haemon man and a small boy standing beside him. I also rushed to my parents and sister, who were running toward me.

Time slowed as they embraced me. No one spoke, although I doubted we could speak through our tears. Just knowing I was with my family again gave me more joy than I could comprehend. I felt like I would burst from having so much happiness inside me.

"You did it, buddy." Dad grabbed my face between his big hands. "You really did it. You defeated the Wraith King."

"But how did you do it?" Mom questioned.

"With help," I added. "I knew Grandpa was right. I was never meant to be the Chosen One, which made me realize there wasn't a Chosen One this time. There couldn't be. The Wraith King killed them all. But as long as there are people in the world who are willing to stand up and fight against evil, good will find a way. And it did. *We* did."

"Gordy, you're brilliant," Mom said with tears in her eyes. "You saved us. You saved us all."

"And I'm not a crow anymore," Kyrie chimed in. "And I can talk again."

We laughed with tears in our eyes, and it had never in my life felt so good just to laugh with my family. When we finally pulled apart, footsteps echoed behind me. Thinking it was Luria or Maharani, I spun around, but I was surprised to see Alexander Bravestone.

"Hey," he said. He scuffed his toe over the ground, then ran his hand through his shaggy blond hair. When he looked up at me, tears sparkled in his blue eyes. "Just wanted to say I'm sorry I stole the sword from you. I should've never done it. I know it was wrong. I was desperate, but I know that's not an excuse. So yeah. I'm sorry." He sniffed and looked intently at the floor, like he was trying hard not to cry. "Really sorry," he added, then chanced a glance up at me. "I hope you'll forgive me."

I hesitated before answering. I'd been so angry at him. I'd been ready to sock his lights out after he'd stolen it, but I'd never heard a more sincere apology, and I wasn't one to hold grudges. "Apology accepted," I said, and held out my hand.

Bravestone gave me a sidelong glance, as if he wasn't quite sure I was sincere. "Really?" he questioned. "You aren't still mad at me?"

"No," I answered, and he gave a visible sigh of relief, then shook my hand with a firm grip.

"It means a lot that you'd accept my apology," he said. "There aren't many people who would be as forgiving as you."

"Well, that's partially because you earned it. I owe you a thank-you, by the way. I know it was you who gave the fake sword to the Wraith King. We would have never stopped him without your help."

"Yeah." He bit his lip and glanced away, as if reliving the moment. "I don't remember much after he turned me into a wraith. It's hard to remember things when you have no emotions attached to the memories. I know that sounds weird. But anyway... when I saw the fake sword get tossed on the ground, a tiny part of me knew it would be important that the Wraith King have that one instead of the real one. If I hadn't so recently been transformed, I wouldn't have known to do it. Part of my human nature was still hanging on." He took a deep breath. "Also, I'm sorry about other things. Sorry about stabbing your dragon. Sorry about the sword. The fake one, I mean. Sorry the Wraith King broke it."

His words reminded me of the weapon scattered in pieces on the ground. A little knot of sadness worked its way into my chest where all the joy had been. I walked to where the remains of Schubert lay, then I knelt beside the pommel. Luria and Maharani made their way toward me, and they knelt by the sword as well.

With gentle hands, I lifted the tarnished silver hilt. It felt so much lighter without the blade. "We couldn't have stopped the Wraith King without you, friend." I spoke in a quiet, reverent voice.

I half expected him to speak up and tell me how noble and brave he'd been. Maybe he'd brag about how he'd single-handedly dealt the final blow to the Wraith King. Or perhaps he'd remark on how he was slightly impressed with a little snotty kid like me. But no, the cavern remained silent.

Luria sniffed, and Maharani vigorously rubbed his eyes.

"Should we... I don't know... bury him?" my cousin asked.

"I've never buried a sword," I answered. "But yeah, that's a good idea. Help me collect all the pieces."

Metal scraped over stone as we worked to collect the fragments. It was hard to believe he was gone; hard to believe I would never hear his voice again. He'd annoyed me for sure, but he'd become a friend all the same, and we would have never defeated the Wraith King without him.

"Nothing a little elbow grease won't fix," a wizardly voice said behind me, and I spun around to face Fandalore himself. A twinkle sparkled in his eyes, and he gave me a quick wink.

"Fandalore," my cousin said in an exasperated voice. "You missed the fight. You missed seeing us stab the Wraith King with the Hero's sword. You missed seeing everyone transform back into people. You missed everything."

"Tut tut," he said disapprovingly. "I may have missed minor details here and there, but I appeared precisely at the moments you needed me."

"Really?" Luria challenged.

"Yes," he said in an equally challenging tone. "If you stop to ponder for just a moment before rushing to judgment, you might realize what you failed to see. I helped in more ways than one, mind you." He stroked his beard. "Care to guess how?"

"You helped by giving us our weapons," Luria stated with a dry, matter-of-fact tone.

"Yes, and...?" he said, drawing out the word.

"You healed Val's wing?" my cousin suggested.

"Yes, and...?" he continued.

"You pointed the way to the Knights' castle where we trained?" Maharani offered.

"Yes, those are obvious answers. What else?" His voice grew more insistent, as if we were overlooking something as noticeable as a giant wart on his nose.

"That's about it," Luria said with frustration. "You didn't do anything else except disappear at random times when we could have really used you—"

"No, wait," I interrupted, then pointed to the gateway leading to where we'd found the magic. "You made sure the Wraith King couldn't get Chorus's magic. It was your spell that protected the magic inside, wasn't it? The same kind of magic you used in the Elderhurst ruins to protect the Hero's sword. You made sure we'd have a chance to stop the Wraith King before he could get the magic out of the cave and turn everyone into wraiths."

"Ah." His eyes lit up. "You've finally guessed it." He patted my shoulder. "Yes, young hero. When the Wraith King first arrived here on this isle, the magic of Chorus called to me as it lay unprotected in this cavern. It was then I knew it would have to be protected if we had any chance of stopping the Wraith King. I rushed here and put up the wards to stop the Wraith King before he had a chance to enter, then I made sure to only allow the wielder of the Hero's sword inside. You, Gordy."

"But why didn't you just make it so that no one could get inside?" I asked.

"Because the Wraith King would have eventually found a way. Better to let it happen now when it was in our control. It all worked out, of course. It always does when there are a few brave people still left in our world who are willing to fight for the side of good and righteousness. Now." He rolled up his sleeves to reveal his skinny arms. "About the business of the sword." He pointed to Schubert's hilt that I still held. "If you'll allow me, I shall repair your weapon. That is, if you wish it?"

I had to swallow a lump in my throat as I held the remains of Schubert. "Well…" I said, pondering the wizard's offer. "I guess it sounds silly, but I'll miss him if he's not around. He may have been rude, but he helped imprison the Wraith King. He deserves a chance. Everyone does."

Fandalore nodded. "A wise choice, young one." He waved his hands over the sword's hilt, then over the pieces that Luria and Maharani held. A soft glow surrounded the sword's pieces, followed by a gentle humming sound. The fragments lifted and melded together with a golden shining light that warmed my face and hands.

The sword, now completely whole again, hovered just above my hands, and I gently grabbed the pommel.

"Well," Schubert exclaimed. "Can you believe it? I died. Yes, me! Praise Chorus. I was in a beautiful, wondrous realm filled with the sweet melodies of a thousand harps. A kingdom of peace and happiness. Filled with laughter and joy and unbelievable happiness. And now… now… where am I now? Back in this dank cave again, I see. In the claustrophobic darkness. With the entombed Wraith King who

recently murdered me only a few yards from where we stand. Ahh..."
He heaved a disappointed sigh. "How lovely."

"You're right," I admitted. "This place is awful. Let's get out of this
stupid cave and escape this island. I don't know about you, but I think
it's time for a very long break."

Chapter 23

THREE, OH, IT'S THE MAGIC NUMBER

In the cool shade of evening, I lounged on the wooden bench in front of my house. Luria and Maharani sat on either side of me. Our front yard had been transformed. Fairies darted around floating glowing lanterns. Chattering voices mingled with the sound of lutes that came from a band of Satyrs playing near the bridge leading to the forest.

My family and friends had all gathered to celebrate the defeat of the Wraith King. Mom, Dad, and Kyrie chatted with Fandalore. The old wizard was explaining that Sir Donald Donaldson had achieved his life's goal and his soul had passed to the hall of statues. Sir John Johnson remained at the circular table in the great hall. Fandalore was planning to pay him a visit soon.

Thimblethorn also lounged nearby, and Uncle Harlowe and Detective Rainwater stood chatting with the big dragon. He was recounting how he'd negotiated peacefully with the red darkfyre dragon to secure a safe ride home for everyone who'd been stuck on Nambour Island. "...more than happy to help after he learned the Wraith King had been imprisoned," he was saying.

Detective Rainwater smiled and gave Uncle Harlowe a playful kiss on the cheek, then he grabbed her hand and threaded his fingers through hers.

"I told you," Luria said when we spotted them still hand in hand half an hour later. Maharani only shrugged at her comment. "About time," was all he said.

A few Haemons had also joined in, including Luria's family and several members of Chieftain Kalize's tribe. It was good to see them laughing and chatting with everyone else.

I took a bite of my fried fudgie and reveled at the taste of warm cream and decadent chocolate. A person could only eat so many nuts and dried fruit in one lifetime before getting sick of them.

"Are you disappointed?" Luria asked me.

I tiled my head. "Disappointed?" I said between bites.

"Disappointed that you weren't the Chosen One," she clarified.

I shrugged. "It doesn't bother me. Being a member of the Chosen Three is way cooler anyway."

Maharani brightened. "We should start our own band," he suggested. "The Chosen Three. Has a good ring to it, don't you think?"

Luria frowned. "I stink at singing. And I don't play any instruments."

"You could use your staff to beat on my shield," my cousin teased. "Like a drum or something. Gordy could be our lead singer."

"Me?" I laughed. "Now you're really dreaming." I took another bite of fudgie. "But you do bring up a good question. What will we do now that the Wraith King is gone?"

"I don't know," my cousin answered. "Go back to our boring lives, I guess."

"Boring?" I questioned. "Life may be boring sometimes, but after getting back from a quest like the one we just had, I'm fine with boring."

"Me too," Luria agreed. "Boring sounds heavenly." She gave me a genuine smile, one that lit up her brilliant yellow eyes that sparkled in the evening sunlight, then she nudged me with her shoulder.

Her hand rested on her knee, and our knuckles brushed as I placed my napkin aside. Maharani cleared his throat. "I'll grab us some more fudgies," he said. "Be right back."

Luria gave me another smile as he walked away. "Hey," she said with a playful jab on my arm.

"Hey," I said back.

"I've got something for you," she said, her eyes bright.

"Got something?" I asked.

"Yeah." She reached down, grabbed her bag off the ground, and pulled out a leatherbound book.

"What's this?" I asked.

"A copy of the Book of Chaos," she answered. "It's an older version. Belonged to my grandpa. It's a little beat up, but I'd like you to have it." She fingered a frayed corner on the corner. "That is, if you want it." She looked at me with expectant eyes.

I reverently took it from her and held it in my lap, then I flipped it open to the first page. Colorful images jumped out at me. The first page showed a white tree with two men standing on either side.

"Chorus and Chaos." Luria pointed at them. "I know your people think Chaos was evil, but I also think his story got so twisted, no one really understands the truth anymore." She gave a nonchalant shrug, although I could see the intensity in her eyes. "You asked what we should do with our lives now. Maybe we should help people find out the truth of the past. Maybe if we do that, then the next time the Wraith King breaks free, we'll be united."

"I like that idea," I said with a smile, and I hoped she heard the sincerity in my voice. "But I can't do this alone. If you're going back to the Haemon lands—"

"I'm not," she interrupted me. "I realize our people living isolated from one another was part of the problem. I've already talked to my dad and my brother, and they've agreed to live here. We've got to stick together from now on. Yes, we've got our differences. But we've got plenty of things in common, too. Maybe if we focus on the good in each other instead of worrying about all our faults, we'll learn to see past them."

"Luria," I said, and finally dared to grab her hand. Her skin was so warm and smooth, it made heat radiate through my whole body. "I haven't heard a better plan in my whole life."

She smiled back, then gave me a quick peck on the cheek. "Good. Because I'm hoping you'll be stuck with me for a very long time."

A very long time. "I like the sound of that."

About the Author

Tamara Grantham is the successful author of more than a dozen books. She's won numerous awards, and many of her novels are number-one bestsellers.

Born and raised in Texas, Tamara now lives with her husband and five children in Wichita, Kansas. During rare moments of free time, she enjoys reading fantasy novels and watching every Star Wars or Star Trek movie ever made.

Also By Tamara Grantham

CHRONICLES OF ITHICAL

The 7th Lie

The End of Never

FAIRY WORLD MD

Dreamthief

Spellweaver

Bloodthorn

Silverwitch

Goblinwraith (novella)

Deathbringer

Grayghost

HARLEIGH SINCLAIR

Harleigh Sinclair and the Raiders of the Lost Ankh

Harleigh Sinclair and Ice Crusade

JUDAH STARWEAVER

Judah Starweaver and the Way of Dragons

LEGENDS OF CRIMSON HOLLOW

Never Call Me Vampire

Dare to Call Me Vampire

THE ALDERFELL CHRONICLES

The Not-So-Chosen One

Don't Blame the Chosen One
TWISTED EVER AFTER
The Witch's Tower
Dragon Swan Princess
Rumpel's Redemption

www.ingramcontent.com/pod-product-compliance
Lightning Source LLC
Chambersburg PA
CBHW060326260626
47160CB00007B/2691